A HORSE
CALLED
MAYONNAISE

JoAnne Collier

REVIEW AND HERALD® PUBLISHING ASSOCIATION
HAGERSTOWN, MD 21740

The author assumes full responsibility for the accuracy of all
facts and quotations as cited in this book.

To Jennifer
who carries the love of horses
into the next generation
and whose enthusiam for the
story kept me going.

Acknowledgments:
Special thanks to Jody and Brandy Mahaffey
for the hours of work they put into manuscript
preparation, to Ken Ferguson and Sherman Hong for
their editorial assistance, and to all my friends
and family who cheered me on.

This book was
Edited by Gerald Wheeler
Cover design by Gert Busch
Typeset: 11/13 Times

PRINTED IN U.S.A.

99 98 97 96 95   10 9 8 7 6 5 4 3 2 1

R&H Cataloging Service
Collier, JoAnne, 1955-
    A horse called mayonnaise.

    I. Title.

                813.54

ISBN 0-8280-0856-6

CHAPTER ONE

Tory stood stock still in the thigh-high fescue, staring. Seed heads bobbed against her bare legs, tapping gently for attention, but she didn't notice.

"I, Tory Butler, am here," she whispered. "Really, actually, finally here." She hugged herself, allowing the deliciousness of the moment to seep through every fiber of her being. This place wasn't just something from a dream—it was a lifetime of dreams merged into one.

A horsefly landed on her shoulder, delivering a nasty bite. "Ouch!" Tory smacked at the spot but missed the fly. It buzzed around her head a few times, then headed for a herd of horses standing in the shade of a huge oak near the barn.

Tory grimaced. "Watch out, guys, here comes the dive bomber." A palomino gelding flicked his ears in her direction but didn't move. He stood head to tail beside a bay mare, his thick creamy tail sweeping around her face then back to his own right flank. The mare's tail brushed his face in rhythm.

"You have a real system going here," Tory laughed as she noticed that most of the herd were teamed up, positioned perfectly to swish flies from areas neither could reach on his own.

"Pretty amazing, isn't it?" a voice broke in from behind. Tory whirled around.

A short, stocky man stood in the deep grass. His freckled skin was burned bronze by what Tory guessed were many days working outside in the sun. A shock of bright red hair lay in a tousled heap on his head, framing a pair of blue eyes.

Tory gulped. "You startled me. I didn't hear you walk up. I'm Tory."

"I'm Mike, head wrangler." The man stuck out a calloused hand. "Glad to meet you, but I've gotta go. Work to do." With a wave, he headed across the field toward the barn.

Since he was the very man she had come to talk to, she ran to catch up to him.

"Mike," Tory puffed. "I want to work with the horses. I know how to ride, and I'm a hard worker. Do you have any openings?"

His eyes suddenly serious, the man paused. "How old are you, young lady?"

"Seventeen."

Brushing a strand of long dark hair from her eyes, she wished fervently that she could say 18. All the summer camp programs she had checked into required its horsemanship staff members to be at least that old.

Mike shook his head slowly. "No, we have our staff already lined up for this summer. Sorry." He started to turn away, then stopped again.

"A hard worker, huh? We can always use a little

extra help around the barn. If you want to spend your free time saddling horses for trail rides and mucking out stalls, come on down."

Tory grinned. "Thanks!"

As Mike disappeared into the dark interior of the barn, Tory could hear him whistling the clear notes of a lively old hymn above the clatter of feed can lids. A horse nickered and stomped its feet. The pungent odor of horse sweat and leather beckoned her to the barn, but she turned away.

The palomino and the bay jerked their heads up to watch her walk by. Two pairs of slender ears flicked forward as if asking for an introduction. Tory approached the fence with an ease of movement and quiet confidence born of years working with horses.

"Hey, you two, I'm Tory. But don't let me interrupt your party," she laughed as the bay mare tossed her head in response. "You're going to see a lot of me this summer, you know. You'll get used to having me around."

The palomino snorted and pawed the ground, his flaxen mane tumbling from a crest so muscular that it caused Tory to suck in her breath in admiration. A rogue forelock tumbled stubbornly over one eye and his sleek coat shimmered like spun gold in the sunlight.

"You are gorgeous," Tory sighed dreamily. "I want to ride you for the pack trip."

The pack trip! She hadn't even mentioned it to Mike. Should she go back and talk to him again? The pack trip was her reason for being here—almost her whole reason for "being" at all. Ever since a friend, earlier in the spring, had told her about the annual week-long trek on horseback into Florida's spring country, she had thought of nothing else.

The cheerful clatter continued somewhere deep inside the barn. Tory shook her head and turned down the path toward the camp's main lodge. She would have plenty of time to talk to Mike about the pack trip later. Glancing back over her shoulder for one last look at the palomino gelding, she saw his head down and eyes half closed, having already resumed his rhythmic tail swishing.

Tory's stomach rumbled. The enticing scent of cinnamon rolls floated through the early morning air. She could see other camp staff converging on a sprawling rustic building that had to be the cafeteria. Following a group of girls through the swinging screen doors, she found herself in a huge room filled with rows and rows of picnic tables draped in bright checkered red and white oilcloth. A handcarved wooden sign hung over the food-serving area: "Take all you want, but eat all you take."

Joining the serving line, Tory tried to ignore her intensifying hunger pangs as she watched those ahead of her piling fried potatoes, scrambled eggs, fruit, and huge frosted sweet rolls, popping with raisins and nuts, on their trays. She turned to the tall, slender girl behind her and whispered, "I think my stomach just quit growling and started barking."

The girl giggled, her blue eyes sparkling. Her shoulder-length auburn hair bobbed as she nodded in agreement. Freckles spattered randomly across her tanned cheeks.

Angel kisses, Tory thought, remembering how much she had hated her own freckles as a little girl until one day her grandma had told her how lovable she must be because the angels liked to kiss her so much.

"My name is Sandy." The girl's soft southern accent broke through Tory's reverie. "You must be new here this summer. I haven't seen you around before."

"I am. I'm Tory. I just graduated from Little Creek Academy in Tennessee and thought Cool Springs Camp would be a great place to earn some money for college. What about you?"

Sandy grimaced. "This is my third summer. I'm a glutton for punishment, I guess. Camp counseling can be pretty tiring. You have kids 24 hours a day for the whole week. They're so energetic. It's rewarding though."

"It must be," Tory laughed. "Three summers in a row. Wow!"

The line crawled forward and Tory finally found herself in front of a huge platter of cantaloupe slices. She took three, glanced up at the sign above the serving area, and took one more. Sandy giggled as she reached for a second sweet roll.

"One thing's for sure, they *do* feed you well. Don't worry though, you *will* work it off."

Trays filled, the girls found a seat near the cafeteria door. "So we can watch everyone come in," Sandy whispered.

"When do the campers arrive?" Tory glanced around the huge room. She couldn't wait to see it filled with 150 12-year-olds.

Sandy popped a section of orange into her mouth.

"Soon enough, dear. Like tomorrow. Enjoy the peace and quiet while you can." She grimaced, but Tory could tell by the expression in her eyes that Sandy was looking forward to the campers' arrival, too.

"By the way, you never told me what you're doing. Are you a counselor?"

"No," Tory sighed. "I'm working in the laundry. But I *really* want to work with the horses. I've already talked to Mike. He said I could help out."

"Oh, Mike. What a great guy. Work you to death, though. Watch him!"

The cafeteria door swung open at that moment and Mike himself ambled into the room, still whistling. A sprig of alfalfa clung to his thick red hair and sweat darkened the back of his blue denim work-shirt. A tall, muscular young man followed him. His jet black hair and drooping mustache caught Tory's eye. Whistling the harmony to Mike's tune, his dark eyes sparkled with the same mischievous light.

Tory leaned over to Sandy and whispered in her ear, "The Frito Bandito, I presume."

The other girl burst out laughing. "You got it, girl," she sputtered, ignoring the curious stares of the other staff members. "Only it's *not* Fritos he steals. Watch out for your heart. That's Brian Winters, Mike's cousin, and he's the assistant head wrangler. At least half of the girls here are in love with him."

Tory stared at her plate. The assistant head wrangler. So Brian would be on the pack trip. And in the barn with the horses. Well, she was one girl who would *not* fall prey to his wiles. Sitting up straight, she squared her shoulders.

8

"Whew, what a determined look." Sandy held a forkful of fried potatoes drenched in ketchup midair and scrutinized Tory's face. "What in the world are you thinking?"

Tory laughed nervously. "Oh, nothing much. I was just thinking about the pack trip and hoping I could help staff it."

"Which one? They'll be taking canoes, backpacks, horses, sailboats off the Keys. . . . A skeleton crew will be staying here and running a program, too. You better sign up soon for the one you want. The sign-up sheet is in the director's office."

Tory froze. What if all the horse pack trip positions were already taken? She pushed her tray back, her sweet roll untouched.

"I've got to go." She swung her legs over the rough bench and stood.

Sandy grabbed Tory's sweet roll and wrapped it in a paper napkin. "Don't forget this." She pointed to the wooden sign and grinned, tossing her the package.

"Right. Thanks."

The sidewalk to the director's office meandered through breathtaking beds of pansies, petunias, and various perennials. The grass lawn sloped gently to the sandy shore of a crystal clear spring. Huge oaks extended moss-draped branches over the spring, as if shielding its tranquility from the outside world. Tory sighed. What a beautiful place to be.

The director's office nestled under a mammoth mulberry tree. The sturdy wooden door creaked as she pushed it open.

A coarse meowing sound drew her attention to a

9

corner of the room. As her eyes adjusted from the sunlight outside, she could see three spotted shapes curled up in a wooden crate. A young man in a neat khaki uniform squatted beside the box. Blond curls fell from beneath his ranger's hat and he wore a pair of heavy leather gloves.

"Hi, I'm Wally Brooks." The young man stood and extended a gloved hand to Tory. "Have you ever held a baby lion?"

"N-n-o-o." She stopped in her tracks. "I can't say that I ever have. I'm Tory." She shook the gloved hand, then leaned over the box. One of the cubs blinked up at her and swatted the air with a furry paw. He hissed as she reached for him.

"Watch it." The warning in Wally's voice stopped her. She withdrew her hand. Wally then slipped the leather gloves from his hands and handed them to her. "Use these. You'll be glad you did." He held his arm up for Tory to see. The sleeve of his khaki shirt had been shredded from elbow to wrist. "They're tough little buggers. Don't let their innocent furry faces fool you."

Tory donned the gloves and picked up the nearest cub. The chunkiness of its little body surprised her. The cub squirmed in her arms and a sharp claw caught her sleeve, slicing it like a razor. She winced as the claw hooked into her forearm, sending a flash of burning pain up her arm. Instantly she dumped the cub back into the box.

"Sorry." Tory glanced up at Wally to see if he was angry. "He got me."

"I see." He grabbed her arm and deftly rolled the

sleeve back. "It's just a nick. Let's wash it out with soap and water, then I'll put some antibiotic ointment and a bandage on it."

He led her to the restroom down the hall and cleaned the wound thoroughly.

"Your friends won't believe you when you tell them how you got this, you know." He laughed as he secured a Snoopy bandaid over the scratch.

With a blush Tory realized that he was still holding her arm. She pulled it back gently. "I have a little trouble believing it myself. When I came over here to sign up for the horse pack trip, I had no idea I'd encounter lions on the way!"

"Anything can happen at Cool Springs Camp, my dear." Wally bowed low in mock veneration. "And the sign up sheet is on the counter by the front door."

"Thanks." Tory giggled. "By the way, Wally, why do you have a box of baby lions in the director's office?"

"They're for the zoo. Haven't you seen our zoo? I'm one of the zookeepers." Tipping his hat, he bowed again. "We have lions, snakes, foxes, llamas, raccoons, baboons, lizards, bats—you name it. It's over behind the staff cabins. Can't miss it. You must come and visit."

Tory bowed in turn. "I would be honored to visit your zoo, Wally. Thank you for the invitation."

Sandy had been right about the sign-up sheet. Under the four different pack trips listed on the sheet were the scrawled signatures of those who wanted to staff them. Tory gulped in dismay as she saw that four others had already signed up for the horse pack trip and quickly added her name to the list. The first name she saw, just under Brian's, was Sandy's.

"That stinker," Tory muttered under her breath. "Why didn't she tell me she'd signed up for the horse pack trip? Why would she encourage *me* to try for it when she knew it would jeopardize her chances of going?" She thought of Sandy's open, friendly face and her thoughtful gesture with the sweet roll. Suddenly she realized that the girl had the potential of being a real friend.

"Sandy, old girl," she whispered to herself, "I hope you get to go even if I can't."

Afterward, Tory wandered down the path toward the spring. Suddenly a piercing shriek split the air just behind her. She whirled around, her heart pounding. A peacock, his neck and breast flashing brilliant blue, strutted across the sidewalk. Another peacock called from its perch on a bench by the spring.

"You scared the stuffing out of me," Tory scolded the bird. "Warn me next time before you yell in my ear, OK?" The peacock sauntered away, his beautiful plumes trailing behind him.

"Beautiful, obnoxious birds, aren't they?"

Sandy stood on the sidewalk with something in her hand, neatly wrapped in a napkin. Grinning sheepishly, she held up the little bundle. "My other sweet roll. My eyes were bigger than my stomach, too."

"Why didn't you tell me you had signed up for the pack trip?" Tory opened her own sweet-roll package and began picking the nuts off and popping them into her mouth as they strolled toward the spring.

"Oh, it just didn't seem important right then.

Besides, two girls get to go. Wouldn't it be fun if you and I both got chosen?"

The morning sun warmed the girl's backs as they sat on a strip of sand by the water's edge. Tory gazed into the depths of the spring, amazed at its clarity. A heavy net stretched across a dark blue area in the spring's bottom. She had heard stories of a cave and a tunnel in the spring where divers had entered, never to return. The thought made her shudder.

Laughter and voices echoed from the path above the spring. A beautiful girl appeared in her bathing suit, a towel draped over her arm. A boy walked on each side of her and several followed behind.

"It must be the Queen of Sheba and her entourage," Tory whispered to Sandy. "Would you look at that hair? And that *tan*."

The girl's honey-colored hair flowed thick and wavy almost to her trim, perfect waist. Her sapphire blue bathing suit sparkled in the sun.

Sandy grunted and stood to leave.

"Well, there goes the neighborhood. Let's get out of here. That's Jan, and she dominates every scene she's a part of. Gets away with it because she's so gorgeous and all the guys like her." Making gagging motions with her finger, Sandy rolled her eyes.

With a snicker Tory followed her up the hill toward the staff cabins. Hearing shrieks of laughter, she looked back to see Jan standing knee deep in the spring, splashing icy water on her fan club.

It must be nice to be so popular, Tory thought. She glanced down at her own white legs. Who had time to tan in academy when every spare second was crammed full with a waiting list of things to do? Then she ran her fingers through her long hair. Fine, straight, limp.

Closing her eyes, Tory tried to imagine what it would be like to have a cloud of wavy hair framing perfect features and a body that boys would follow around.

"Tory!" Sandy's voice cut through the fantasy. "Did you hear anything I said?"

"Uh, no. I guess I didn't. Sorry."

"I was saying I think you should know Jan put in a request to go on the pack trip. She signed up right after me."

Tory stared at Sandy.

"What?" She tried to picture Jan mucking out a stall, but the only image she could conjure was of her sitting sidesaddle in a gossamer gown, her golden hair floating in the breeze. Tory groaned.

"I guess I may as well give up on the pack trip. Competing against you and Jan is too much for this little country girl." She sank to the ground in a heap.

Sandy grabbed her hand and pulled her to her feet.

"Don't be silly. I'll bet you're a hundred times better with horses than Jan. Looks aren't everything, you know."

"Thanks," Tory said with a wry smile. "I feel better already."

"Don't mention it." Sandy smacked her playfully on the back. "Come on. Lets find our cabins."

CHAPTER TWO

Tory tossed in her bunk, dreaming she was on safari in Africa and a glorious sunset streaked shades of rose, peach, and gold across the vast sky. The camel she rode had a long flaxen mane and tail like one of the camp horses. Each jarring step the camel took, threatened to shake loose the rope saddle Tory had cinched to his hump.

A lion roared beside the path. Then another and another. To Tory's horror, each lion had a human face and all of them were Jan's! The lions closed in as the saddle slid precariously to the side of the camel's hump. Tory screamed.

"Tory. *Tory.*" A hand on her arm shook her awake. She could see Sandy's worried eyes peering at her through the morning darkness. The lions were still roaring, though.

"What is that racket." Tory sat up in bed and rubbed her eyes.

"The lion cubs—they just want their breakfast— they're hungry." Sandy perched on the end of Tory's bunk. "You were yelling in your sleep."

Tory slipped out of bed and grabbed her jeans.

"Yeah, a nightmare. I'm just not used to having lions in my backyard."

"I came over to wake you anyway," Sandy said, brightening. "Mike sent a message for you to come down to the barn if you want to go on a trail ride. The campers are coming in today, and he's taking a group of them out."

"Great!" Tory grabbed her boots and slipped them on. After running a brush through her hair, she reached for her shirt.

"Here. Let me help you with your hair." Sandy took the brush and divided Tory's hair into sections, deftly braiding it. "There. You look the part, now. Go gettem', Annie Oakley."

It was already hot for so early in the morning. Accustomed to cool Tennessee mornings, Tory felt sweat beads popping out on her forehead as she jogged across the field toward the barn. Her riding boots sank into the loose sand, slowing her down.

Mike and Brian were already leading saddled horses from the barn to the hitching post. Swinging her arms casually, Tory tried to look nonchalant as she approached the barn. If only she could stop that annoying pounding in her heart.

"Hiya, Tory," Mike called, leading a sleek black gelding from the barn.

"Hi," Tory waved shyly, suddenly feeling very conspicuous. She watched Mike wrap the gelding's reins around the hitching post. The horse snorted and pawed the ground, his muscles rippling under his glistening ebony coat.

Tory whistled softly to herself. That had to be

Midnight. She'd heard about him from the other staff members. A hunk of a horse. Maybe if she couldn't have the Palomino for the overnight pack trip, Mike would assign Midnight to her.

As the head wrangler sauntered into the barn for another horse, Tory raced to catch up with him. "What can I do to help?"

Mike scratched his head. "Hmm. Let me think. How about saddling the horses in the two end stalls and taking them out."

She nodded, noticing that someone had placed each horse's saddle on the gate to his stall. A bridle hung from each saddlehorn.

A familiar equine head poked over the half-door of the last stall. Wide set, intelligent eyes gazed from a golden face. A metal name plate fastened to the stall door read "Toby."

"So you're Toby, huh." She fumbled with the latch until she got it open.

The palomino gelding appeared even more magnificent up close than from a distance. Grabbing a curry comb from the top of the stall wall, Tory brushed the horse's sleek coat until it shone. Toby pushed her with his nose as she reached for the saddle blanket.

"Too bad, old boy", Tory chuckled. "You're not getting out of work today." After throwing the saddle blanket onto Toby's withers, she then slid it down toward the middle of his back. She didn't want the hair on his back pushed the wrong way, irritating him all day.

Toby stood politely while Tory heaved the saddle up onto his back and tightened the cinch. She patted his neck affectionately."You sure are a sweetie," she whispered as she led him out to the hitching post. "I hope I get to ride you today."

The horse in the other end stall, a slender little strawberry roan, shied when Tory entered. As she flattened against the far wall, her ears flicked back and forth nervously.

"It's all right girl," Tory crooned. "Come on. Let's get the saddle on."

The little mare calmed as Tory kept up a soothing monotone, moving slowly and carefully so as not to spook her. It wasn't until she had the mare saddled and turned to unlatch the stall gate that Tory noticed Brian observing her silently from the next stall where he curried a chestnut mare.

"Uh, hi." He seemed embarrassed that Tory had caught him watching her. "I didn't say anything because I didn't want to spook Jasmine. You did such a great job of calming her down. I'm Brian. And you must be Tory. Mike told me all about you."

Tory met his gaze coolly.

"Nice to meet you, Brian." She opened the gate and walked past without another word.

Campers poured across the field toward the barn as Tory led the mare to the hitching post. While she rubbed the velvety muzzle, Jasmine nibbled her sleeve affectionately.

"You're a sweetie, too." She kissed the roan's cheek. "I'll be glad to ride you if I can't have Midnight or Toby."

"Tory, could you help us mount up these kids, please?"

Mike had already started matching campers to the horses. Tory helped a chubby little girl clamber up onto Big Jim's broad back, and held the reins of a skittish bay mare for a grinning, freckle-faced boy.

"This one's a short trail ride," Mike yelled to her from the front of the line. "Grab a horse and help us if you want to."

She noticed that he was riding Toby. When she glanced around at the other horses she saw a girl with new riding boots perched on Midnight's back, and a serious looking boy neck-reined Jasmine into the line.

Tory tried to ignore the disappointment that welled up inside her. After all, she had plenty of other horses to choose from. But she looked around quickly and discovered, to her dismay, only one horse remained riderless.

Henry.

His head hung low as if he were too tired to hold it up, and his lower lip sagged. Every bone of his huge frame showed through the loose skin draping his body.

Swallowing hard, Tory blinked back the tears. But throwing the reins over the old horse's head, she mounted up.

Brian, on a feisty little bay named Buckshot, led the group single file along a winding sand path that bordered the camp grounds. Buckshot pranced and sidestepped, chomping at the bit. Frothy flecks flew from his muzzle with each toss of his head.

Midnight followed, Miss Shiny Boots tall in the saddle. Tory chuckled to herself as she watched Midnight respond perfectly to every aid used by the girl. She had heard that he was fierce and fiery with an experienced rider, but now he was calm and placid when small hands held the reins.

Directly behind Midnight, Jasmine minced along, an Arabian princess straight out of Scheherazade's tales. The somber boy handled her well, giving her just enough head to protect her sensitive mouth but not enough to allow her to bolt. He was the perfect rider for the flighty young mare. Tory could see her calming with every step.

An albino gelding followed Jasmine. Jugheaded Barney delighted in plodding, head down, straight into Jasmine's hindquarters. When she nickered and kicked him in the chest, he blinked his pink eyes in feigned surprise. Seconds later he resumed his tailgating, much to the consternation of his pig-tailed young rider, who shouted threats and sawed at his reins in a futile attempt to control her stubborn mount.

The freckled boy astride the bay mare reined in behind Barney and just ahead of Tory on Henry. A shock of bright red hair, almost the shade of Mike's curly thatch, jutted from his head, Alfred E. Newman style. Mischief danced behind his smile, but Tory noticed a gentleness in his interaction with the mare.

There's a boy that has known some pain in his life, Tory thought. She marvelled at the insight Mike had displayed when he matched campers with horses. The bay mare was obviously perfect for the boy. Somewhat flighty and frightened, in need of reassurance, but stable and responsive to his reaching out. They brought out the best in each other.

She could say the same of every other horse and

rider in the line. Jim, the gentle giant with hoofs the size of cannon balls, lumbered along directly behind her. The chubby little girl, her pink cheeks glowing, giggled joyously with every rolling step the huge draft horse took.

Mike and Toby brought up the rear. If Toby's muscular body looked wonderful in the field as he relaxed and grazed, it was incredible to behold saddled and bridled, every muscle flexing under the knees of an experienced rider. Tory glanced down at Henry's bony hindquarters and ridged back and sighed.

The trail snaked through thick patches of palmetto, tropical plants that looked like miniature palm trees but sported rows of vicious "teeth" on their stems. Quickly Tory learned to prop her legs on the pommel of her saddle to keep the razor-sharp fronds from biting into her skin.

Henry never flinched, never spooked, never responded in any way to Tory's movements. He just shuffled on. Soon Tory began to enjoy the freedom he offered her to think about other things. The whole line traveled at the pace of the slowest rider, so it didn't matter that Henry was no racehorse. And she certainly didn't have to be on her toes to keep him in line. Her mind drifted back to her first horse.

Chief.

A gift from her parents on her twelfth birthday, Chief was a dark bay with a crooked white blaze and four white, spotted stockings.

"He's an appaloosa," her dad had joked the day she got him. "His blanket just slipped down around his ankles."

To Tory, he was a dream come true, a companion and a confidant. She spent hours after school and on Sundays wandering the countryside on Chief's sturdy back. He seemed almost to read her mind and to sense when she was hurting or lonely. Tory was glad that the campers also had opportunity to experience a bonding with some very special horses.

"She'll be coming 'round the mountain when she comes . . ."

The chorus burst into Tory's daydream. Mike's Irish tenor joined Brian's rich baritone voice, and the two soon had the entire line of campers singing. One song followed another as campers yelled their favorites. Tory laughed and sang until her jaws ached.

Brian turned frequently to check the line of riders for any problems. Tory made sure she was always looking the other way when he did. She had to admit that he *was* terribly good looking and had one of the most beautiful voices she'd ever heard. But she certainly wasn't interested in being a member of his silly fan club.

The trail ride ended too soon. Smiling campers piled down from their horses when the group reached the barn again. They chattered excitedly about how much fun they'd had and made plans to return another day to ride again.

Tory led the horses one by one into the barn to unsaddle and rub them down. The air was hot and sultry enough to make man or beast sweat, especially if the beast wore a saddle.

The rest of the day passed quickly. Tory mucked out some stalls, oiled bridles, sprayed the barn floor with a fine mist of water from the hose to keep down the dust, and did other odd jobs around the barn. When the huge old school bell rang to summon the staff and campers to the evening meal, she turned to leave.

"Oh, Tory," Mike called from the tack room, "thanks for helping us out today." He poked his head out the door and grinned. "And by the way, we'd like you to help us out on tomorrow's overnight pack trip. I've already called up to the director's office to get you cleared from laundry duty. Interested?"

She gulped. "Interested? Sure!"

"Good. See you at 6:00 a.m." Mike ducked back into the tack room.

Tory almost floated to the cafeteria. It was too good to be true. And maybe tomorrow she could ride Toby or Midnight.

CHAPTER THREE

The oaks stood black against the pale morning sky. Spanish moss hung like some giant's laundry from their massive branches. As Tory hurried to the barn, a knapsack, stuffed with a change of clothes and some toiletries, bounced from her shoulder.

Mike was already saddling horses, whistling a cheerful tune.

"Hi." He smiled when he saw Tory. "You're here bright and early. That's good. Help me saddle up, and I'll tell you which horse you're riding today."

Tory thought she detected a suspicious twinkle in Mike's eye, but started saddling horses without comment. Mike had brought some new horses in from the back pasture. He must have come down early to trim their feet. Curled up chunks of hoof lay scattered over the breezeway floor she had swept clean the evening before. Grabbing a rake, she pulled the scraps to the side, making a mental note to sweep them up later and throw them into the compost pit.

Before long, the campers arrived, each eager to know which horse would be his or her's for the trip.

Brian pulled up in Mike's station wagon with

supplies for the pack horses to carry. Tory watched quietly as Mike assigned horses. Her heart sank, as one by one each of her favorite horses went to some-one else.

"Oh, Tory." The head wrangler's forehead wrinkled as he studied the rumpled sheet of paper in his hand that listed all the horses and their designated riders. "I'm giving you Walker."

She stared at him in utter disbelief. Old bag-of-bones Walker? He made Henry look like a thorough-bred. Tory held her breath waiting for Mike to tell her it was all a joke, but he had already turned away, helping campers with their packs.

Slowly, Tory fastened her pack to Walker's saddle. The old horse swung his sagging neck around and peered at her through rheumy eyes. She patted his flank and climbed into the saddle.

Mike boosted the last camper into the saddle and swung up on Toby's back. He reined his horse toward the trail, then stopped, dismounted, and trotted into the barn. Seconds later he reappeared carrying a broom.

"I almost forgot this," he said, handing it to Tory. "Stick it on the back of your saddle somehow, OK?"

Tory gulped. A broom of all things! She felt her neck flushing scarlet. Where would she put it? Finally, as the line pulled out of the hitching area, she shoved the broom between her pack and the back of the saddle. It stuck out on each side.

"What a ridiculous sight I must be," she muttered to herself as she urged Walker into his place in line.

As the day wore on, she became more and more convinced that Walker's name was perfect for him.

No matter what the pace of the other horses, he plodded along at his own slow speed. If he saw a tempting clump of grass that he wanted to sample, he just stopped altogether, and no amount of pulling, tugging, and coaxing could budge him.

The saddle-weary group finally reached the overnight camp site. Tory was relieved to climb down from Walker's back. She took off his saddle and bridle and led him to the nearby river for a drink. Then she brushed him down and turned him loose in the makeshift camp corral Mike and Brian had constructed on a previous trip.

As she put the brush away, Tory noticed Mike watching her. He grinned, then turned to help a camper unsaddle. Tory hurried to the cook's tent to see about supper.

Brian sat cross-legged on the floor of the tent, a pile of macaroni and cheese packages scattered at his feet. He was opening a huge can of Heinz vegetarian beans with an old camp can opener that screeched and groaned with every turn of its rusty metal handle. He looked up, relief on his face, as Tory entered.

"Could you give me a hand here?" He pointed to the macaroni and cheese. "Dinner."

Her sense of duty prevailed over her urge to run. She turned to hide the red creeping up on her neck. "Sure, but let's get some help." Poking her head out the tent door, she called to a little group of campers relaxing by the fire. "Anyone who wants to eat, come help with the work!"

Before long, a big pot of beans bubbled over the fire. The odor of macaroni and cheese drew the campers to the kitchen tent like bees to a flower. Tin plates and cups rattled in anticipation.

Mike stood by the fire and watched the campers fill their plates. Then he raised his hand for silence. "Let's pray."

His voice rose and fell in beautiful cadence as he asked God to bless the food. He prayed for each individual camper by name and even mentioned a mare back at camp that was due to foal any day. It was almost as if Mike were carrying on a conversation with God, forgetting that anyone else was present at all. Tory half expected to see God standing there beside him when she opened her eyes.

That night after supper, while the group followed Mike and Brian on a moonlight hike, Tory sat by the campfire watching the sparks dance up into the darkness. She thought of how differently the pack trip had turned out from her fantasy. Instead of riding a horse with a lot of class, she'd gotten stuck with Walker. Determined to make a good impression with her riding ability, she hadn't been able to make Walker even pretend to obey her. And that broom!

Then she smiled to herself. The trip had been fun despite everything. Especially working with the campers. They were a great group.

When she heard footsteps behind her, she turned to see one of the campers walking up the path from the river, his hair dripping. He sat on the log beside her and stuck out a hand. "Hi. I'm Todd. I don't think we've officially met."

Tory shook the extended hand solemnly. "I'm Tory. It's an honor. Why aren't you on the hike with the others?"

His huge hazel eyes lit up as he flashed her a smile. "I was. I just took a shortcut back so I could take a dip in the river." He pulled a bunch of daisies from behind his back and handed them to her.

"For the world's most beautiful horse woman." Tory blushed as she took them, their petals shimmering in the firelight. Daisies had always been her favorites.

"Thanks, Todd," she said finally. "For the flowers and the compliment."

"I'm sincere." He tossed a pine knot into the campfire. It hissed and popped like a living thing. "I've been watching you all day. You're probably the only person on earth who could make Walker look classy."

Tory laughed. "That's a lost cause for sure. Especially with a broom stuck across the back of the saddle."

"That was a test, you know," he said quietly.

She stared at him. "What do you mean, 'test'?"

"Just that." He assumed a conspiratorial tone and leaned closer. "You want to go on the week-long pack trip, don't you?"

"Well, y-yes," Tory stammered, "But what does that have to do with Walker? And how did you know that I wanted to go on the pack trip?"

Todd laughed. "That one was easy to figure out." He picked up a twig and began drawing stick figures of horses in the sand at his feet. "You're spending every spare minute in the horse barn volunteering your extra time to help out. You're on this overnight pack trip, which I happen to know is a test. And besides that," he grinned mischievously, "I saw the sign-up sheet for the pack trip."

"You stinker." She eyed him skeptically. "Why are *you* so interested in the pack trip anyway?"

"I'm going on it, of course. I signed up months ago. I'm 13 now, so I'm old enough to go. Last year I was too young to be in teen camp."

"All right!" Tory beamed. "It'll be great to have you along. That is, if I get to go." A mosquito whined past her ear. She gave it a chance to land on her arm, then smacked it.

The boy threw another knot on the fire. "I'd say your chances are better than average. Jan came on this very same trip last week. Mike matched her up with Walker, too. And gave her the broom to carry. She was horrified and complained the whole time."

Tory gulped. "Jan? Perfect Jan rode Walker? I can imagine her on Midnight or Toby or even Buckshot, but never on Walker."

"Well, apparently *she* couldn't imagine herself on Walker, either. The real high point came when she broke one of her nails. You'd have thought the stock market had just crashed."

Todd snickered, obviously enjoying the memory. Then he frowned. "The only problem is that Brian likes Jan. All she has to do is flip that head of hair around, and he's cornmeal mush."

Tory giggled. "I'm sure that that's never happened to you, has it?"

The boy fluttered his thick eyelashes in feigned surprise. "Who, me? Never!"

Laughter and voices floated through the night air, and Tory could see bobbing flashlight beams coming up the path along the river. Mike's high-pitched voice rose above the others. It sounded like he was telling a knock-knock joke and no one was listening.

"The troops are returning." Tory stood and stretched. "Thanks again for the flowers, Todd."

"Sure." He grinned up at her. Then his face clouded and a look of anguish flitted across his eyes. "Tory"—he stared at his knuckles for several long seconds before speaking—"can I talk to you sometime? I need to talk to somebody."

Something in his voice disturbed her. It was such a contrast to their previous light-hearted bantering.

"Sure, Todd. Anytime. We can talk now if you want to. Do you want to take a walk?"

The boy shook his head. "No. Another time, thanks. I'm going to bed. I'm exhausted." He got up and disappeared into the darkness.

Tory still stood gazing into the night when the rest of the group arrived seconds later. Brian smiled in greeting when he saw her standing by the fire.

"Hey, thanks again, Tory, for the help with supper. I was feeling a little overwhelmed at first. But everything turned out great."

"Sure, no problem. Goodnight, everybody." She turned toward the path to her tent. Hundreds of stars glittered overhead. A meteor flashed across the velvety night sky.

"Does this mean I get my wish, God?" Tory whispered. "I know this will be a real newsflash, but the most important thing to me right now is to go on that pack trip."

A whippoorwill called plaintively in the distance

as she climbed into her tent. A gentle breeze rustled the leaves of a willow at the river's edge. The horses milled quietly in the makeshift corral, settling themselves in for the night.

As she snuggled down in her sleeping bag, an old saying floated through her mind: "If you love something, let it go. If it comes back to you, it's yours. If it doesn't, it never really was."

Tory thought of how intensely she had been focusing on that pack trip for the past few weeks. It had become almost an obsession.

"OK, Father," Tory said quietly. "I'll let it go. I can have a great summer whether I have that particular opportunity or not. I give it all to you."

When she thought of Jan, she realized to her surprise that the jealousy had faded. With a contented sigh she drifted into a deep, dreamless sleep.

CHAPTER FOUR

H ey, I told you I wanted my shirts folded *this* way."

Tory flinched as Wesley, one of the camp lifeguards, snapped a T-shirt in her face. Then he threw a stack of shirts on the table in front of her. "Now fold them right."

She pushed the pile back to him. "Fold them yourself. Your mother doesn't work here."

Then she turned and grabbed a hose to fill one of the old wringer washers she used to do the staff's laundry. Fighting the urge to aim the spray directly at him, she kept her back turned until she heard the laundry hut's door slam behind the muttering lifeguard.

With a sigh she added a cup of bleach to the load of socks she was washing. This job was certainly less than romantic. Just then she heard a chuckle behind her and whirled around, hose in hand. The cold spray caught Wally directly in the face as he walked through the door.

"Watch it!" he sputtered, laughing as Tory, horrified, redirected the hose into the old washer. Grabbing a towel from the dryer, he swabbed his face. "*I'm* not going to tell you how to fold clothes. I think it's amazing that anyone takes time to fold them at all. Wadding them up and cramming them in the drawers is so much less complicated."

Tory stared at him.

"Sure I heard it. I was right outside the door. Great comeback! That guy thinks he's so cool. He needs a humbling experience or two to balance his perspective."

She giggled. "I just wish I'd hosed him down instead of you. What's up?"

Wally held up two masks, with matching snorkel and fins. "How about some adventure to break the monotony of your humdrum existence?"

Tory peered into the churning mass of socks, then glanced over at the piles of dirty laundry waiting to be washed.

"Give me two hours and I should be done for the day. Will you have time for a swim then?" She grabbed a sock and poked it through the rollers into a tub of clean rinse water.

Wally grinned. "Sure, I'll be back in a couple hours. I have something special to show you."

For the next two hours her hands flew, separating colors from white, checking name tags, washing, wringing, rinsing . . . wringing, drying, folding . . . She actually enjoyed the challenge of transforming limp, dirty rags into crisp clean clothes.

Most of the staff responded gratefully to her efforts. Wesley, of course, was an exception, but she tried to ignore him, chalking his insufferable behavior up to a bad attitude. Tanned, with a gorgeous head of wavy dark hair, Tory knew he could be one of the most popular staff members at camp if it weren't for his caustic remarks and lack of respect for others. Shaking her head, she turned her thoughts to a more pleasant topic.

In the three days since the overnight pack trip, Tory had seen little of Mike and Brian or the horses. Catching up on her laundry duties had left no time or energy for volunteer stable work. Aching to know who they were considering for the pack trip, she determined to ask Brian about it at supper.

Wally returned just as Tory folded the last pair of jeans, hot from the dryer. "Ouch!" she yelped, jerking her hand back from a scorching hot snap. "These dryers are like ovens."

Wally grabbed her hand and held the burn under a stream of cold water in the sink, then broke off a piece of an aloe vera plant that grew in a pot on the window sill. Peeling back the skin of the succulent spike, he rubbed the red spot with the green gel.

"There," he said smugly. "Good as new."

"Yes, doctor," Tory laughed. "It'll be fine now. Where are my mask and snorkel?"

The spring teemed with shrieking, splashing campers. Wesley sat in one of the tall white lifeguard chairs, a brass whistle dangling from a cord around his muscular neck. His jaw tightened and he turned his head away as he saw Tory and Wally approaching.

"What's so special here?" Tory ignored the lifeguard and stared at the crowded spring.

Wally held his finger to his lips, motioning for her to don her gear and follow him. He dove into the clear water and swam away from the spring hole toward a narrow outlet almost hidden by overhanging tree branches and tall reeds. Tory plunged in, gasping as the icy water enveloped her. She peered through her fogged mask, searching for Wally, but dozens of thrashing arms legs and heads obscured her view. Holding her breath, she continued paddling toward the spot where she'd last seen him.

The spring narrowed, approaching its outlet. The deep iridescent blue of the water gave way to a clear green. Delicate aquatic plants undulated in the gentle current, tickling Tory's legs as she swam through them. Brightly colored fish darted in and out among the fronds. A snapping turtle soared gracefully through the watery shadows like an alien spacecraft searching for a landing site.

Tory gazed around her in fascination, breathing rhythmically through the snorkel. She felt as if she had entered another world, another dimension where time and gravity lost their power and weightless movement reigned supreme.

A pair of feet appeared on a submerged log directly in front of her. She raised her head out of the water to see Wally balanced precariously on the log, holding his fins.

"I thought I'd lost you, slowpoke," he teased. "What do you think of the scenery under there?"

Tory whistled in appreciation. "It's like a fairyland. I love it."

"Well, I have something else to show you. Follow me." He struggled back into his fins, adjusted his mask, and slipped into the water with Tory close at his heels.

The stream turned, flowing through a heavily wooded area. Wally stopped abruptly and reached for what appeared to be an underwater ladder. Then he pulled himself up the ladder and out of the water. She gasped.

A treehouse straight out of Robinson Crusoe towered above her. Rope bridges connected rustic parapets. Three mammoth oaks served as its foundation with numerous small apartments nestled in their branches.

Tory pulled the fins from her feet and scrambled up the ladder. The lowest level of the treehouse had the most wide open space.

"For campfire programs," Wally explained, "without the fire, of course."

The second level housed the kitchen and dining areas. Shelves, strewn with old spice tins and plastic containers, lined the kitchen walls. Tory followed him through the dining area and up a swaying rope bridge to the next level. She held her breath as she gazed out at the dense forest surrounding the treehouse.

"Wow," she whispered, "*this* is an incredible place."

Wally grinned. "I thought you'd like it. It's always been pretty special to me." He glanced at his watch. "Uh, oh, we'd better get back. Suppertime."

"Yeah, I need to make it to supper tonight." Tory frowned, "I want to talk to Mike and Brian about the horse pack trip."

Wally studied her face thoughtfully. "You look worried. Do you think someone else is going to beat you out of your spot?"

"What spot?" Tory sighed dramatically. "Jan and

Sandy both signed up before I did. Jan is gorgeous and a conference president's daughter, and Sandy's been here for three summers and knows everyone. What chance do I have?" She felt the old anxiety rising up from deep inside.

Taking her arm, Wally steered her back down the narrow rope bridge to the main level. He was quiet until they reached the ladder that disappeared into the river, then he turned and looked her squarely in the eyes, his hands on her shoulders.

"You, young lady, are underestimating yourself. Tell me, what are your qualifications for going on this pack trip?"

"Well, uh . . ." she stuttered, taken aback by the sudden shift in the conversation.

"Come on, Tory, I'm sincere. I want to hear them. Resumé time."

"OK. I'm a good rider. I can handle any of the horses at the barn. I like kids and enjoy teaching them how to ride. I'm a hard worker. I'm not afraid to get my hands dirty."

"Good start," Wally smiled. "Tell me more."

"I get along with the other staff. I have a positive attitude and strong spiritual values. I can usually think clearly in an emergency situation . . ." Her voice trailed off.

"All right. Good enough for now. Work on that list. Remember that Tory is a unique and valuable child of God with a lot to offer in life. Don't limit her."

She laughed. "OK, OK." Wriggling loose from his grip on her shoulders, she plopped down on the deck to pull her fins on. "So, sir, when are you going to set up a counseling service?"

He laughed and shook his head. "Not me. I'll stick with animals, thank you. They're not nearly as complicated as humans. Besides, *you* don't need a counselor. You just need to learn to believe in yourself."

Tory leaned thoughtfully on a wooden post. "I know you're right. I don't *want* to be jealous of Jan. But although I've tried to surrender it to God, it still ambushes me sometimes." Tory sighed and pulled her mask on, balancing it on her forehead. "She seems to get anything she wants without even trying because she's beautiful and popular. It's not fair."

"Nope. It's not." Wally sat down to pull his fins on. "But don't sell Mike short. He sees a lot more than you think he does. You and Sandy are much more likely to get picked than Jan."

"I'd *love* to go with Sandy." Tory's flippers slapped on the wooden surface as she waddled to the water's edge, preparing to jump in for the icy swim back to camp. She glanced over her shoulder at him and thought she detected a look of longing flit across his face when she mentioned Sandy's name.

"Hey, Wally. What are you thinking?"

The expression vanished and he grinned sheepishly. "Nothing. We need to get back to camp if we're going to make it for supper."

Campers and staff had packed the cafeteria by the time Tory arrived. Wally had already gone through line and was sitting at a table near the massive fireplace with several of the lifeguards, his plate piled high with spaghetti.

Grabbing a tray, Tory took her place in line.

Swimming in cold water always made her hungry. Tonight she felt like eating everything in the kitchen. She glanced up at the sign over the serving deck and made a mental note to take only what she was sure she could eat.

"Tory!" Sandy's head bobbed out of the line ahead of her. She left her place and came back to join her. "Where have you been? I looked all over camp for you this afternoon. I wanted to tell you I found out the pack trip announcements will be made tomorrow at supper."

"Great!" Tory pulled a fork from the silverware container. "I was with Wally. We swam down to the treehouse. Have you been down there?"

Suddenly the same look of longing she'd seen in Wally's face hovered in Sandy's. For a second she glanced away, but when she turned back, the light-hearted sparkle had returned to her eyes.

"That's great. The treehouse. Unbelievable, isn't it? And Wally's a super guy, I'm glad you had a good time." She started to turn away again. "I think I'll skip supper tonight. Spaghetti is so fattening, you know."

Tory caught her arm. "Just a minute here. What is it with you guys? This is the same reaction I got out of Wally when I mentioned your name today. What's going on?"

Sandy stared at her. "I don't know what you're talking about. I'm perfectly happy for you. Not jealous at all. Just because you're going out with Wally doesn't mean you and I can't be friends."

"W-What?" Tory stuttered. "I'm not going out with Wally or anyone else. Besides, I think he's in love with you and afraid to admit it. Judging by your reaction, you have the same problem. Wally and I are friends. Period."

Sandy laughed nervously and glanced around to be sure no one was listening. "So I overreacted and gave myself away, huh." She dumped a huge mound of spaghetti on her plate. "Wally and I dated for a little while last summer. I was crazy about him, but he backed off and never told me why. He's avoided me ever since."

"I'm sorry." Tory squeezed her friend's arm sympathetically. "I'm here if you ever need to talk."

Sandy flashed a smile, tears glittering in her hazel eyes. "Thanks. That means a lot."

Tory's mouth watered as she filled a bowl with tossed salad and piled her plate with spaghetti and garlic bread. Once through line, she scanned the crowded room for Brian and Mike. It was her last chance to make an impression before they announced the final decision. She remembered Wally's words that afternoon at the treehouse and squared her shoulders.

She couldn't see Mike at all, but it didn't take long to spot Brian's dark head bobbing as he talked to several of the off-duty counselors and a female lifeguard who shared the table with him. Holding her breath, Tory started toward his table.

Just at that moment the front door of the cafeteria opened and Jan floated in, her thick golden hair billowing behind her. Her bronzed skin glowed in the lamplight, a perfect contrast to her white jumpsuit cinched tight at the waist with a gold sash.

Tory's stomach twisted into a knot as the girl approached Brian's table and slid onto the bench beside him. Although Tory wasn't close enough to hear what she said, she did see Brian's face light up as Jan slipped her arm through his, leaning her head lightly on his shoulder.

Tory set her tray, untouched, on the nearest table and ran out the door, letting it slam behind her. Tears rolled down her face as she stumbled to her cabin. It was no use. She could tell by Brian's face that Jan would go on the pack trip and Tory would wash her dirty socks when she came back. That's how it always turned out anyway. Someone else always won. She was never good enough. Never quite good enough . . . Tory curled up on her bunk and cried herself to sleep.

CHAPTER FIVE

A lion roared and Tory rolled over in her bunk. She kept her eyes shut tight, not wanting to know if it was morning or not. Not wanting to even face the day and its inevitable disappointment.

The screen door opened, than shut lightly. Tory lay perfectly still, hoping whoever had entered would see her sleeping and leave. She heard a rustling beside her bed . . . then suddenly, tiny paws forced her mouth open and began probing around inside it as she felt the weight of a small body on her chest.

With a shriek she flung the furry creature off her bed and sat bolt upright. As her eyes adjusted to the thin morning light, she could see a pair of bright black eyes peering at her from the corner of the cabin. It was a young raccoon, chirring softly as if reassuring himself.

"You imp!" Tory exclaimed. "What on earth were you trying to do to my mouth? That was a rude awakening, you know."

The raccoon padded back and forth along the cabin wall. He had either forgotten how he got in or was in no hurry to leave. After pulling on her jeans and a T-shirt, Tory squatted down a few feet from the restless animal.

"Come on, little guy," she cooed. "Come to mommy, and I'll take you home." She held her hand out, palm open. The raccoon stood up on his hind legs, sniffing as if to check the hand for food. When he realized it was empty, he stretched out and nipped the end of one of her fingers.

"Ow!" Tory jerked her hand back. The bite hadn't broken the skin but it was quite a pinch. "OK, tough guy. You asked for it. I'm going to have to call in the big guns." She slipped out the door, closing it securely behind her, and ran down the path to the zoo.

Wally was in the zoo kitchen, preparing breakfast for the lions. He looked up, surprised, when she burst through the door. "Where's the fire?"

"No fire." Tory collapsed on a chair to catch her breath. "But I have a friend of yours in my cabin. He seems to be an expert on breaking and entering. In fact, he's even dressed for the part, mask and all."

Wally groaned. "Oh, no. Not Bandit. I've been keeping him in an outdoor cage because he wreaks havoc when he gets loose inside." He looked out the window to the courtyard where an empty wire cage stood. "That little Houdini! So he ended up in your cabin, huh? Well, I'll have to say he has good taste in people."

Ignoring her look of consternation, Wally grabbed a small wire cage and headed out the door, Tory close at his heels.

Bandit ran to him as soon as he opened the door, climbing his pant leg as if it were a tree trunk. Wally scooped the creature up and poked him in the cage. "There, you rascal. It's back to the penitentiary with you. And no paroles."

Bandit reached through the wire mesh to touch Wally's shiny belt buckle. His tiny paws, like little hands, worked constantly, and he kept up a continuous soft chirring.

Tory walked with Wally back to the zoo.

"I think I'm going to call my folks and ask them to come get me today," she said, kicking a pine cone down the path with the toe of her sneaker.

Wally stopped and stared at her. "What?"

"Just what I said. I want to go home. Washing dirty laundry all summer isn't what I had in mind."

Wally shifted the cage to his hip, sending Bandit tumbling. The raccoon caught his balance and released a volley of angry chirrs obviously directed at Wally.

"Sorry, little guy." He reached a finger through the wire and scratched Bandit behind the ear, then continued in silence until he and Tory reached the zoo building. There he transferred Bandit back to his cage and turned to Tory.

"I'm sorry to hear you say you want to quit," he said quietly. "I don't want to tell you what to do, but I wouldn't be much of a friend if I didn't let you know what I think." He rubbed his chin thoughtfully. "I think you're making a mistake. If you give up now, you'll never know what might have happened had you hung in there. The things that are worth doing don't always come easy. You have to take risks, hanging in there even when things look bleak."

Then he gave her a sidelong glance and grinned,

suddenly self-conscious. "That was a sermon, wasn't it? I'm sorry. I know you have to make your own decision, and I'll support you in it, whatever it is."

Tory sighed. "Life gets a little complicated sometimes, doesn't it?" She turned to leave. "I'll go down and clean some stalls. That always helps me think more clearly."

Suddenly she looked up at him. "Can I ask you a personal question?"

"Sure. I guess. I'll decide after you ask it if I want to answer it or not."

Tory hesitated, then plunged ahead. "I know its none of my business, but why did you and Sandy break up last summer?"

Wally stared at his feet for a long time, shuffled uncomfortably, then cleared his throat. "Somehow I know I'm going to regret talking to you about this but it won't be the first time I've shot myself in the foot, so here goes . . ." he laughed nervously.

"Sandy is a super person. Best there is, in my book. She has a great personality, high ideals, intelligence, good looks . . ." The sadness returned to his face. Pulling a blossom from the mimosa tree that grew in the courtyard, he twisted at the threadlike pink petals one by one as he talked.

"I was afraid of disappointing her. Of not being good enough for her."

Tory started to protest but he held his hand up to silence her.

"My background is rougher than hers. I've made mistakes. She's done so well that I just felt like I could never measure up. We spent a lot of time together at first, then when our relationship was obviously progressing to something more serious, I stopped seeing her."

"Just like that? You didn't talk to her? Explain to her how you felt?"

Wally shook his head slowly. "Not a word," he said miserably. "How could I explain something like that?"

"Easy," she smiled encouragingly. "Just like you're telling me now. She would have understood." On impulse she reached over and squeezed his arm. "She'd understand now, I think, if you'd just talk to her." Grinning impishly, she added, "Of course you have to make your own decision, and I'll support you in it whatever it is, but . . . I'm going to tell you what a good friend once said to me:

"'You are a unique and valuable child of God with a lot to offer in life, and you need to learn to believe in yourself.'

"He also said, 'If you give up, you never know what might have happened had you hung in there!'"

"Remind me never to give you advice." He threw a mimosa blossom at her.

Tory laughed. "You just need to learn to listen to yourself. Now go feed your lions. I'm going to the barn to work off my frustrations."

No one was in sight when she arrived at the stable. The clear sky offered no cloud cover to reduce the sun's merciless rays, so the cool cavernous barn was like an oasis from the hot sand of the road.

Tory grabbed a pitchfork and shovel and attacked the first stall. It felt good to put herself into the task, twisting and stretching as she pitched manure and dirty hay from the stall floor and replaced it with clean bedding.

The horses were all out to pasture. She could see them through the open door at the end of the barn, standing idly in the shade, flicking flies from each other as they had when she first arrived. Leaning on the pitchfork, she watched them, remembering that day and how simple everything had seemed then.

"That's a pretty serious face, there, youngun'."

Mike stood in the breezeway, a bright red bandanna tied around his forehead.

"I-I didn't know anyone was around. I came down to work off a little steam."

The head wrangler rubbed his chin thoughtfully. "A little steam, huh? Mucking out stalls is a good way to do that. One of the best, I'd say. You've got a manageable area to work with, it requires enough umph to burn any pent-up frustration, and there's just enough manure to remind you of how bad you feel in case you start to forget what you're there for."

Tory laughed. "I've just done one stall and feel better already. It must work."

Mike headed for the tack room and soon reappeared, his shoulders piled with bridles and harness parts. He held a can of harness oil and a handful of old rags. "Wanna help me oil these bridles?" Sitting on a wooden pallet, he held a bridle up to her.

"Sure, I'd love to."

Tory sat on the pallet, leaned her back against the wall of one the stalls, and began oiling the bridle. The oil soaked into the leather, making it a rich mahogany color.

Mike labored in silence for a long time, his able fingers working the leather. Finally he spoke.

"I had a young horse once. I had high hopes for that horse. Higher than for any horse I've ever known. All day I imagined how I would train him, and all night I dreamed of riding on his back."

Setting the bridle aside, he took another from the pile. "I worked with him day after day. When I tried to halter him to teach him to lead, he bit me. And when I tried to trot him in circles on the lunge line, he bolted and got away from me. I had to chase him for hours to get him back." Mike chuckled to himself.

"He was a corker, that one. He kicked me when I hazed him to get him used to the saddle. Stomped on my foot when I tried to teach him to pick up his hooves for the farrier. When I climbed onto his back for the first time, he bucked and crow-hopped like a rodeo bronc. I hit the ground so fast I wasn't sure which way was up!" Mike slapped his leg and shook with laughter. "I rode him out in an open field the next time, but he ran away and raked me off on a tree branch. Then stopped as if nothing had happened and waited for me to get up and climb back on."

Tory listened, wide-eyed, to his story. It was hard to imagine him having that much trouble with any horse. They all seemed innately to respect him. Mike leaned over and looked her straight in the eye.

"Do you know who that horse was?"

She shook her head.

"Toby. Good old Toby." He chortled again.

"Toby?" she gulped, "he's one of the best horses

in the barn."

"I know. Knew it then, too. Sometimes success is hidden behind a whole string of failures. Sometimes you just have to gut it out."

Tory stared at the bridle in her hands. "How did you know I was thinking about quitting?"

Mike chuckled softly and threw her a clean rag. "I've been around a while, kiddo. I know the look when I see it. It's the what-am-I-here-for-when-somewhere-life-must-be-easier-and-a-lot-more-fun look. It's most often seen on the face of someone leaning on a pitchfork or a shovel. *I* sure had it some of those early days working with Toby."

Tory sighed. "That's the second 'don't quit' sermon I've gotten today. Do you suppose somebody is trying to tell me something?"

"What do you think?" Mike pushed the bandanna up on his forehead and grinned.

"Could be." When she stood to stretch her legs, he tossed her several of the oiled bridles.

"Hang these in the tack room for me, could you, please, then I've got something I want to talk to you about."

Tory found the appropriate hook for each of the bridles, returning to settle back down on the pallet. She waited expectantly to hear what he had to say.

Mike labored quietly, taking great pains to work the fragrant oil into every inch of the bridle. Tory knew better than to interrupt. He would speak when he was ready.

"I brought a young gelding in from the upper pasture the other day." Mike said finally. "A paint.

Good breeding. He should be a great trail horse." Reaching for one of the clean rags, he wiped the oil from his hands.

"Problem is, I don't have time to train him. He's almost four and hasn't had a hand laid on him. Green as grass."

Tory caught her breath. Could Mike be saying what she thought he was? Her heart pounded.

"What do you think, Tory? Would you like to train him?"

The huge room seemed to spin in circles. Tory could have sworn the wooden pallet they were sitting on was floating a foot off the ground. She gulped and realized he was waiting for an answer.

"Yes. Yes!"

"Good." Mike grinned. "I'll bring him in this afternoon and you can start anytime you want to. I'll help you of course."

Her imagination soared. She pictured herself in buckskin, proudly trotting through camp on an Indian war pony. A majestic paint, his chocolate brown spots spread like a map over his muscular frame.

"Tory." His voice was insistent, as if he had called her several times already. "Do you want to see him? He's in the pasture behind the barn."

"Sure!" She jumped up and followed him out the back door to the grassy field where the horses stood, half asleep.

"There." Mike pointed to a little gray and white gelding barely bigger than a pony. "His name is Mayonnaise."

"Mayonnaise." Her mouth hung open as she

stared at the wrangler. "Where in the world did he get a name like that?" Her heart sank as her dreams faded before her eyes. This was no Indian war pony.

Mike grinned proudly. "Oh, I named him that. Fits him, don't you think?"

Looks like he has a little horseradish there on the side, Tory thought, but just nodded in agreement.

Mike stuck his hand out. "Do we have a deal, young lady? Want to train him?"

A surge of excitement began to push aside the disappointment. Grabbing his hand, she shook it. Mayonnaise *was* a horse, and it would be a good experience to train him. What could she lose?

CHAPTER SIX

Lunch over, Tory hurried back to the stables.
Mayonnaise stood quietly in the first stall,
munching on a bucket of oats Mike must have given
him when he brought him in. He looked bigger up
close. About 14½ hands, she guessed.

Slipping into the stall, Toby ran her hand along
the young gelding's withers. He stood calmly without
shying or flinching. Then she stepped back a few
paces and studied his conformation.

The line from the point of his shoulder to his
withers sloped nicely. His chest was well developed
for such a young horse. Close coupled and well-
ribbed with solid, straight forelegs, he had the under-
pinnings of a good trailhorse. His neck was well set,
strong and arched. Large, prominent eyes, clear and
alert, were set wide apart in a fine-boned face.

Tory patted the paint's neck admiringly. "You
are a good horse."

Then she left to collect her equipment and give
Mayonnaise time to finish his oats. When she returned he was just licking the last grains from the bottom of the bucket.

For Mayonnaise's first lesson, Tory brushed his coat all over with several different kinds of curry combs. She combed his creamy mane and tail until they shone like satin. After brushing his belly and legs down to the fetlock and pastern, she picked up each hoof to clean it with a hoof pick. Throughout the procedure Mayonnaise's sensitive ears flicked, listening to every word Tory said, picking up on every sound, but he never protested.

"You like this, don't you?" she whispered, amazed that a horse with such minimal handling would be so gentle. She reached for the halter she had placed on top of the stall wall and slipped it over the gelding's muzzle. He snorted and backed up a few steps, then stopped.

Tory kept up a constant stream of conversation with the horse, talking in an even, calm voice, low-pitched and soothing. She could sense Mayonnaise responding to its sound and her firm but gentle touch.

Snapping a lead shank onto the halter and pulling lightly on the lead rope, she opened the stall door. Mayonnaise's ears perked up in surprise. He took a few steps into the barn's breezeway, then stopped short. Tory tugged but met resistance. She knew better than to pull straight forward when a horse planted his feet and refused to budge. Realizing that she wasn't strong enough, muscle for muscle, to outpull him, she knew she'd have to outwit him.

Turning the horse's head to the right, Tory got him to take a step. Then she directed his head to the left so that he advanced another step. Finally, when she pulled straight forward, he followed quietly, the picture of obedience. She walked him out into the hitching area, around the posts into the corral, then back into the barn to his stall.

"Wow, I think I could try a saddle on you today." She pulled a carrot she'd saved from her lunch out of her pocket and gave it to the gelding.

"Sure, go for it. You're doing great." Tory turned to see Mike watching her from the doorway. "In fact, stay put, and I'll bring it to you."

"Thanks!"

He handed her the saddle blanket first. "Haze him a little, see how he does."

Tory held the saddle blanket out and let Mayonnaise smell it. Then she flapped it gently all over his body—withers, neck, chest, flank, legs, and hindquarters. He pranced nervously when she first started but soon realized he had nothing to fear and stood quietly, following the movements with his ears.

After resting the saddle blanket on the paint's back, Tory reached for the saddle. The leather creaked and Mayonnaise shied as one of the stirrups flopped against his belly. Tory set the saddle down and ran her hands gently along the horse's neck, talking quietly, reassuring him.

Mike entered the stall.

"Here, let me hold him while you saddle him. It'll give him more of a sense of security."

The wrangler kept a tight hold on Mayonnaise's halter while Tory picked the saddle up again, heaving it lightly to the gelding's back. Mayonnaise gathered himself for a crowhop, trembled, then relaxed. Tory reached under for the girth strap and fastened it loosely. She stepped back and grinned at Mike.

"There he is. What do you think?"

"Great work. You're a natural, kid."

"I'd like to lead him around outside for a while with the saddle on and get him used to the weight."

Mike nodded in agreement, and Tory led the horse from the stall. She had to admit he looked great saddled. She tightened the cinch slightly, enough to keep the saddle snug but not enough to panic the gelding, and walked him down the road toward the tennis courts that bordered the far pasture.

Two girls bounced a tennis ball back and forth across the net as Tory and Mayonnaise approached the court. The girls wore crisp white tennis outfits that accentuated their tanned legs. Feeling suddenly awkward, Tory glanced down at her grimy jeans and sweat-stained shirt. "You don't care what I look like, do you, old boy," she whispered to the animal.

The horse nudged her with his nose as if in answer. Tory giggled.

"I sure like you. I think we're going to have some great times together."

As she turned Mayonnaise back to the barn, Tory glanced up and realized one of the girls playing tennis was Jan. She looked different with her hair tied back. When she saw Tory, she waved and smiled. Tory waved back.

"Nice horse," Jan called. "Can we see him?"

"Sure." Tory stopped and waited as the girls ran across the grass to the sandy road. She was amazed that Mayonnaise didn't spook at all at their approach. Instead he stood quietly while they petted him, talking excitedly.

"I want to go on the pack trip so badly," Jan said, a look of longing on her face. "My dad doesn't want me to—he's afraid I'll get hurt, but it would be so much fun. I get tired of living in a glass bubble." She turned and looked at Tory as if really seeing her for the first time. "Are you going on the horse pack trip?"

"I-I don't know," Tory stammered. "They'll announce the staff for the trips tonight. I want to."

Jan was even more beautiful up close than from a distance, but Tory noticed something about her that she hadn't seen before. Maybe it was because there were no boys around to distract her. Or maybe it was just a mood. But an empty, lonely look haunted Jan's eyes.

"I've got to get Mayonnaise back to the barn. I'd better go," Tory said finally. "See you later. Good luck, Jan."

Jan smiled. "You, too," she said in a tone that seemed sincere.

Tory's thoughts whirled as she headed down the road with Mayonnaise in tow. It was strange, but somehow she felt sorry for Jan. Always before when she had tried to imagine what it would be like to be so beautiful, she had thought in terms of its benefits. Any disadvantages it might have had never entered her mind. How would it feel to never be secure that you were valued because of who you were and what you had to offer instead of just because others wanted to be seen with you? What would it be like to have all the other girls dislike you just because you were born with an unusually pretty face?

She realized with a sense of shame that she had been doing exactly that. That she had been judging Jan and shutting her out on the basis of physical characteristics beyond the girl's control. Prejudice against someone's skin color or national origin had always disgusted Tory, but she knew her dislike of Jan's beauty sprang from the same roots: selfishness, ignorance, and fear. She shuddered.

"Father," she whispered. "I thought I'd surrendered my jealousy of Jan to you, but I guess I didn't go deep enough. I don't want just my behavior to change so I'm a 'nicer' person. I want your unconditional love for her."

As she led Mayonnaise into the hitching area, Mike was spraying down the entry way. He looked up as they approached. "Hey, that must have been a great walk, judging by the look on your face. Quite a different expression than the one I saw this morning."

Tory laughed, "It was a great walk." Leading Mayonnaise to the stall, she gave him another handful of oats. She was about to uncinch the saddle when Mike's face appeared over the stall door.

"Do you want to try riding him today? I think he might be ready, he's taking to all this so easily."

She stared at him. "Really? You think it would be OK?"

"Sure." He chuckled at her eagerness. "Go for it."

Tory tightened the cinch to keep the saddle from sliding. When Mayonnaise rolled his eyes and pranced a few steps, Tory softly and soothingly reassured him. Mike handed her a hackamore to replace the halter, so she would have reins for control but the young gelding would not have to get used to having a bit in his mouth along with everything else he had encountered that day. Then Mike led him to the hitching area.

"OK, kid. Mount up." He grinned at her. "I'll hold him while you get on."

Tory held her breath and slipped the toe of her boot into the stirrup, then swung her leg lightly over the paint's back in one fluid motion. As soon as she settled in the saddle, she kicked her toe loose from the stirrup and gripped the gelding's sides with her knees to keep her balance. She had seen riders dragged by a foot caught in the stirrup of a panicked horse. It hadn't looked like something that she ever cared to experience.

Mayonnaise stood still, trembling. Tory kept up her monologue, saying whatever came to her mind just so the horse could hear her voice. She stroked his neck gently. Mike still held the reins, watching for any signs that the young gelding was about to bolt. He led the horse in a small circle to allow him to adjust to the sensation of having a rider on his back.

"Well, it looks like he's ready for the next step. Are you?" Mike handed Tory the reins and stepped back.

"Sure," Tory said, teeth clenched.

Leaning on a hitching post, Mike crossed his arms. "You're on your own, kid."

Squeezing her knees against Mayonnaise's side, she made a clucking noise to signal the horse to move. She knew the horse would not know what she meant, but she wanted to use such signals from the start to teach him properly.

Mayonnaise took a step. Then two. Then everything exploded. Tory felt the saddle heaving under her. She grabbed the saddle horn and squeezed tightly with her legs to keep from being thrown off. Tears blurred her eyes as the world spun around her.

Then, as unexpectedly as it had started, the bucking stopped. Mayonnaise stood still, his sides heaving and his neck drenched with sweat. Tory pressed her knees into his sides again and clucked. This time he stepped forward obediently and followed the path around the corral, docile as a lamb.

Hearing cheering and whistling, Tory glanced back at the hitching area to see Brian standing beside Mike, a huge grin on his face.

"Way to go, Tory," Mike shouted. "That was some real riding."

Tory gave the thumbs-up signal and turned Mayonnaise into the field. To teach him to neck rein, she pulled gently on one rein, while firmly resting the other over his neck. The young horse responded surprisingly well, as if trying to understand what she wanted him to do.

She reined the gelding back toward the barn. "You deserve the world's best rub down," she murmured, smoothing the horse's sweat-caked neck.

Once back in the barn, she pulled the saddle and hackamore off and returned them to the tack room. Then she curried Mayonnaise's coat until it shone and cleaned his hooves thoroughly.

When Tory was sure the gelding had cooled down sufficiently, she gave him a long drink of cool water and turned him out into the pasture. He immediately stopped and rolled in the sand until it covered him head to hoof. Then he stood up and shook himself as if to say, Whew, I'm glad that's over.

Tory laughed. "A lot of good that rubdown did. You look like a ragamuffin now."

Mayonnaise snorted and joined a group of horses lounging in the shade of a huge maple. Reluctantly Tory turned away. It had been a great afternoon, and she hated to see it end. Then she remembered. The pack trip announcement! They would make it tonight at supper. Already she could hear the clanging of the supper bell and knew that the moment she'd been waiting for was almost here. Would she be going on the pack trip? She gulped. Did she really want to know the answer?

CHAPTER
SEVEN

Tory ran down the sandy road toward the cafeteria. Her heavy riding boots slowed her progress, so when she reached the sidewalk she sat down quickly, yanked the boots off, and hurried the rest of the way in her socks.

Ignoring the curious stares of campers congregating on the cafeteria porch, she plopped down on the steps to pull her boots on, then hurried inside to find a table.

The cafeteria hostess was already dismissing tables one by one so Tory knew the group had already sung the blessing song. She slid into an empty place at one of the staff tables just as the hostess motioned for those sitting at it to go through line.

As she maneuvered her legs back out over the bench, she glanced up and realized that Sandy and Wally were seated directly across from her. Sandy smiled broadly and Wally winked at Tory, a self-satisfied expression on his face. She shot him a questioning look, but he just shook his head slightly and held a finger to his lips.

Standing directly behind the couple in line, Tory

watched the way he touched Sandy's arm and knew something had happened. She smiled to herself.

Fresh fruit, grilled cheese sandwiches, and boiled eggs made up the supper menu. A large bowel of mayonnaise sat beside the egg tray. Tory scooped up a large dollop to mix with her egg. She smacked her lips and sighed. "Mmm, my favorite supper."

Wally glanced at the pile of mayonnaise on her plate and shook his head in mock dismay. "I can see you're controlling your fat intake well, Tory. You probably only have 30 or 40 grams there."

She laughed. "Mind your own business, bub. I'll watch my fat intake tomorrow. Eggs with mayonnaise are my favorite."

The group settled back down at their table just as Elder Miller, the camp director, walked to the front of the room and cleared his throat. Everyone immediately fell silent.

"I'm sure you're all eager to know who will be staffing the pack trips. The assignments have been made, and I would like to share them with you now."

He pulled a sheet of paper from a folder he had been carrying and began to read.

"The canoe trip, headed up by Scott Winters, will also be staffed by Wesley Smith, Debbie Freeman, and Jill Novick."

Wally leaned across the table and whispered to Tory, "Scott is Brian's brother. He requested for you to go on the canoe trip, but I guess he didn't get his wish."

Tory shuddered as she thought of what it would be like to spend a whole week with Wesley. She wondered how Scott even knew she existed, then remembered one day the week before when she had paddled a canoe around the spring just to maintain her skill level. Scott had been there, too, and had commented on how well she handled the craft.

Elder Miller read the names of those chosen for the backpacking trip. Tory didn't recognize any of them. She just breathed a sigh of relief that she wasn't on the list.

"Now for the horse pack trip, headed up by Mike and Brian Winters. Supportive staff chosen are Sandy Pearson and Tory Butler."

Tory heard Sandy gasp. The room began to whirl as she tried to absorb the reality of what she had just heard. "I'm going," she whispered. "Going on the pack trip. The pack trip!" She felt tears running down her cheeks and grabbed her napkin to mop them up. Glancing up at Sandy, she saw her doing the same thing.

The girl's eyes met in one moment of unparalleled joy. "Yes!" they mouthed to each other, then turned to hear the rest of the assignments.

Jan sat at the next table over, her face registering disbelief and disappointment. Three trips had been announced and she had not been on any of them. Suddenly Tory felt a surge of sympathy for her.

"The last trip is a sailing expedition off the Bahamas," Elder Miller grinned as surprised whispers rippled through the room. "This is the first year we've tried a trip like this. We'll see if it's worth repeating in future years. The trip will be led by Wally Brooks and James Mann with Jan Cole and Teresa Dunlap assisting."

Tory jerked her head around to stare at Wally. His eyes twinkled as he folded his arms across his chest. She could see Jan out of the corner of her eye, laughing and crying at the same time, talking excitedly to the others at her table.

"You knew," Tory whispered across the table to Wally. "You knew all along that Sandy and I were going on the horse pack trip and that Jan was going sailing, didn't you?"

He just shrugged his shoulders and laughed.

Elder Miller clapped his hands for silence.

"You're all welcome to resituate yourselves so you can meet with your group and begin planning your trip if you like."

Tory grabbed her tray and stood up to scan the crowded room for Mike. Locating his red hair across the dining room, she made a beeline for his table, Sandy close at her heels.

Mike stood quickly and bowed. "Hiya, crew." He motioned for them to sit down. Brian nodded politely in greeting, obviously more intent on eating his supper than on discussing the pack trip. Tory wondered if he was disappointed that she was going instead of Jan. If he was, it didn't show on his face.

Mike raised his hands to get the little group's attention amid the noise. "Let's pray together before we get started."

Tory bowed her head, closed her eyes, and listened while Mike talked to God about the pack trip. He requested wisdom for the group as it planned for the trip and asked that the outing would be of spiritual benefit to each camper participating. Again Tory was amazed at the sincerity and simplicity of the wrangler's prayers. *It's like God is his best friend,* she mused. *I like that.*

Until Mike's prayer she hadn't thought of the pack trip as a spiritual journey. She had seen it only as an adventure, a chance to experience something new and different.

"We'll have great opportunities on this trip to teach spiritual lessons." Mike said, as if reading her mind. "Some of these kids are really hurting. Getting out in nature and working with the horses will give us all a prime environment for learning and growth."

The two girls nodded thoughtfully, almost forgetting to eat. Tory glanced down at her plate of almost untouched food. Brian had already emptied his and headed back to the serving line for seconds. As she picked at her sandwich, she remembered the sign over the serving area and determined to eat it anyway.

Brian returned, his plate piled high with fruit and sandwiches. Mike shook his head, then turned to Tory, pointing at the heap of mayonnaise on her plate. "So you like a little egg with your mayonnaise, huh?"

Brian laughed heartily as she nodded. She stared at her plate as she felt herself blushing. Why did she blush so much around him?

Mike produced a notebook and a pen. "OK, guys. All seriousness aside. Let's get down to business." His face was solemn, but a little twitch at the corner of his mouth gave him away. The girls giggled.

The group spent the next two hours planning the pack trip. Tory was amazed at the number of decisions needed to pull off a trip of its magnitude. Tory and Sandy pored over menus and grocery lists while Mike and Brian listed the necessary supplies to care for horses, staff, and campers for a week in the woods. They drew a map of the proposed route and made plans to contact each landowner for permission to cross and/or camp on his property. If any one property owner refused access, they would have to change the whole route.

Twelve campers had signed up altogether for the pack trip. Mike passed the list around for everyone to see. Tory was pleased to see Todd's name on the list. It would be great to see him again. She thought of the flowers he had given her on the overnight pack trip and smiled. At the same time she remembered his request to talk to her and made a mental note to be sure to create an opportunity on the week-long trip.

She thought how it would be great to work with Sandy. The girl's enthusiasm made even the most tedious task seem fun. Glad they'd both been chosen, she glanced over and caught Sandy leaning back, smiling dreamily to herself.

"I'd give a dollar for that thought," Tory said playfully, poking her friend in the ribs. Sandy jumped, startled.

"Oh," she said, with a sheepish expression, "I was just thinking about Wally." She hesitated, making sure the rest were absorbed with their planning and not listening. "We had a long talk yesterday. It was great." A wistful look crossed her face. "I wish he could come on the pack trip with us."

"You mean instead of the sailing trip with Jan?" Tory said in a teasing voice.

"Yes, well, er, no," she stammered, her cheeks flaming. "Not exactly. It's not that. I just hate to be separated for a week, now that we've just gotten back together."

"Well, if it's Jan that's bothering you, I can assure you that Wally's head will never be turned by her," Tory chuckled. "I have inside information that you're the only one that can accomplish that."

Sandy sighed. "Thanks, Tory. I guess I needed to hear that right now. I don't want to be jealous."

Tory smiled grimly. "Nope, no fun. Doesn't accomplish a thing, either."

"I know you're right." Looking over at the table where the sailing crew gathered in intense discussion, she sighed again.

"I want to let go, but how do you do it? Sometimes I feel like I'm being pulled apart."

Tory nodded sympathetically. "I know that feeling." Suddenly she remembered a book she'd once read. "Have you ever read *Hinds Feet on High Places* by Hannah Hurnard?"

Sandy shook her head.

"It's great." Tory stood up to carry her plate to the dishwashing area. "I recommend it highly. It's a parable. The girl in the book wants so badly to get to the spiritual high places, out of the reach of fear, pride, and selfishness. She learns a lot on her journey about letting go." Tory grinned. "Reminds me a lot of you and me."

On impulse Sandy hugged her. "You're a good friend, Tory Butler."

"I know," Tory giggled. "I can't help myself."

At Mike's request, both girls arrived at the barn early the next morning to help organize equipment for the pack trip. To Tory's surprise, Mayonnaise stood saddled and tied to the hitching post. Mike and Brian sat nearby, repairing some old bridles.

"I thought you'd like to work Mayonnaise a little while it's still cool," Mike said casually as he punched buckle holes in a new throatlatch strap he'd made for one of the bridles. "I'd like you to take him on the pack trip if you can get him broken in by then. You'll have two weeks to work with him. He's catching on so fast I think you can do it."

Tory stared at the paint, then back at Mike. She couldn't believe he had so much confidence in her training abilities. But she knew, given time, Mayonnaise would be a perfect trail horse.

"Sure!" She untied the hackamore reins from the hitching post and flipped them gently over his neck. "I'd love to ride him on the pack trip."

Tory poked a toe into the stirrup of Mayonnaise's saddle and started to swing her leg over his back, then stopped short. There taped to the seat of her saddle, was a boiled egg. Both men howled with laughter at the look of surprise on her face.

Mike stood up and stamped in circles, laughing and slapping his legs. "You said you liked egg on your Mayonnaise, so here it is," he hooted, wiping his eyes. Brian and Sandy laughed until tears ran down their faces.

Tory swung to the ground, grabbed the egg from the saddle, and threw it at Mike. She missed and hit Sandy instead.

Confused by the commotion, Mayonnaise snorted and tossed his head.

"It's all right boy." Tory hugged the gelding's neck. "They're just a crazy bunch. Of course, you and I are perfectly normal. We're going along on the pack trip to add some semblance of sanity to the group, right?"

The paint pawed the ground with a foreleg. "See?" Tory exclaimed. "He agrees with me."

"Right." Sandy made a face. "He did that just to shut you up. Mayonnaise knows full well that you're as crazy as the rest of us!"

Mike chuckled as he threw several of the bridles over his shoulder and headed for the barn. "OK, guys, we've got a lot to do before the trip. We don't have much time to get ready." He stopped and turned to Tory. "Go ahead and work him a while."

She swung lightly into the saddle and reined Mayonnaise into the corral. It was a perfect place to do figure eights and circles—great practice for neck reining, leg aids, stops, and starts.

"I can't believe the pack trip is almost here," she whispered to the horse as she cantered him in a tight circle. "And you and I get to go together." Tory shuddered as she thought of how close she'd come to quitting.

Pulling Mayonnaise to a walk, she marveled again at how quickly he responded to her requests. He seemed eager to please her. She remembered her longing to ride Toby or Midnight on the pack trip. Now it had disappeared completely, eclipsed by the pleasure of riding a horse she was training herself—

especially a horse as well-mannered as Mayonnaise. When she thought of Mike's uncanny ability to team up horses with riders, she laughed out loud.

"We're quite the pair, you and I." She reined Mayonnaise toward the barn. "The matchmaker has done it again."

CHAPTER EIGHT

Tiny spiderwebs sparkled with dew in the early light. The peacocks shrieked their wake-up calls. Tory took a deep breath of the cool morning air, then stepped back inside the barn. Already she'd been awake for hours.

She led Buckshot to the hitching rail, groomed and saddled. His chestnut coat glowed.

"Today is the day, my friend." she shivered with excitement. "I wonder who will be riding you for the pack trip?" The horse nuzzled her pocket. She laughed. "How did you know I had something in there?" Producing a lump of sugar, she held her palm out for him to lick it up. His tongue felt warm and sticky on her hand.

"You'll spoil him."

Todd stood on the other side of the hitching rail, grinning mischievously. Dressed in faded old jeans and a chambray shirt, he had a denim knapsack slung over his shoulder.

"I didn't hear you walk up. You ready for the pack trip?"

"You bet." He walked with her back into the

barn. Mike was leading Jasmine out to the rail.

"Hiya, Todd." The wrangler slapped the boy on the back as he passed him. "You're early. Wanna give us a hand here?"

Todd's face lit up. "Sure! What can I do?"

"Saddles and bridles are on the stall doors. All the horses need to be groomed and saddled up by the time the rest of the campers arrive."

The boy headed for the nearest stall almost before Mike finished his sentence. The wrangler winked at Tory. She could tell he was pleased by Todd's eagerness to help. Sandy and Brian emerged from the tack room carrying the packs that each rider would fasten to the back of his saddle.

"Quite a worker, that one." Sandy nodded in Todd's direction. "I hope they're all like him. It'll make our week a lot easier."

Brian shook his head. "Don't count on it. If I've learned anything from working with kids, it's that they're a lot like horses. Some will go all out to please. Others are jugheaded and stubborn, like old Barney. You almost have to threaten them with bodily harm to get them to do anything." He sighed heavily. "And some have been abused as youngsters and are frightened and confused. It takes a lot of patience and consistency to win their trust."

Tory slipped into Midnight's stall and began to curry his black coat, Brian's words still running through her mind. The pack trip no longer appeared to her as just another adventure to tell her grandkids about someday. She was beginning to see it the way Mike viewed it: as a ministry, a chance to reach out and share God's love with a group of kids at a very important time in their lives.

Throwing the blanket and saddle over Midnight's glossy back, she tightened the girth. As she fastened the throatlatch of his bridle, she pushed a black forelock from his face and stared him straight in the eye.

"You be good this week, Midnight," she said sternly. "I'm counting on you. You're not the star of the show—you're a teacher. Understand?"

Midnight shook his head and pushed at Tory's pocket. She pulled out a small lump of sugar and held it out to him. "OK. It's a deal then?"

A small face with beautiful brown eyes appeared over the stall door.

"Is this Midnight?"

Tory opened the door and led the horse out into the breezeway. The girl stood on tiptoe, her eyes shining. Her long dark hair was pulled into a neat French braid.

"I'm Carol, and Mike told me I'd be riding Midnight."

Tory smiled and handed her the reins. She watched them as they walked out to the hitching area. They were a striking pair.

"Look who I'll be riding." Todd led Merrilegs, a stout little Welch cross, feisty enough to give any of the bigger horses a run for their oats.

"Two peas in a pod, you two are." She patted Merrileg's neck affectionately and grinned at Todd. "He has a lot of heart, you know."

Todd bowed solemnly. "Thank you, my lady. I take that as a high compliment, comparing me to this noble steed." Then he laughed as he led Merrilegs outside.

A slightly chubby girl with thick wavy blond hair and sky-blue eyes tugged at Barney's girth strap. "He's holding his breath and won't let me tighten it," she said, a note of frustration in her voice.

"Here, let me help." Tory led Barney in a small circle, then stopped and quickly tightened the cinch. "There you are." She handed the reins back to the girl "It's kind of hard to hold your breath and walk at the same time. We just outsmarted him."

"Thanks!" the girl smiled, her face lighting up. "I'm Connie." She pointed to Carol, already astride Midnight. "That's my twin sister."

Tory saw something flickering in Connie's eyes as she apparently waited for her to comment on how different she looked from her sister. Turning away from Carol and Midnight, she said, "I'm Tory." She pulled a burr from Barney's mane. "I'll be one of the staff on this trip. Just don't let this old boy give you any guff." After helping another camper with his pack, she stopped and looked back at Connie. "You know, Connie," she said quietly, "you have the most beautiful eyes I've ever seen."

Connie's face registered shock, then a pleased expression replaced the look of disbelief. "Thanks." She smiled shyly and busied herself with her pack.

A tall boy, tanned and handsome, was fastening a pack to Toby's back. He muttered angrily to himself as the pack shifted in spite of his effort to tie it on straight.

"Need some help?" Tory stood back, waiting for

some indication that he would accept her assistance.

"No," the boy said flatly. "I can do it if this dumb horse would just stand still."

Tory watched the animal, his feet planted solidly, never moving a muscle. She stuck out a hand. "I'm Tory, one of the wranglers."

The boy shook her hand reluctantly, obviously focused on the task at hand. "Donnie. Glad to meet you."

"Same here, Donnie. Let me know if I can help." As she walked away, shaking her head, she thought of Brian's comment about people and horses. "This guy should be on Barney," she mused.

All 12 campers were now present and accounted for. Tory moved from horse to horse, assisting with packs and offering encouragement. She noticed that Brian and Sandy were doing the same. Mike had disappeared.

A rumbling in the distance caught her ear. Big Jim, the huge Belgian, appeared over the hill, pulling a brightly painted green and red buckboard. Mike held the reins and clucked to Jim, urging him on. The buckboard was piled high with supplies for the week. Boxes of canned goods, bags of grain for the horses, and baskets of kitchen utensils bumped and clattered with each step old Jim took.

The campers cheered as Mike and Jim approached with the buckboard. Brian did a last minute check to make sure all cinches were tight and packs secure. He frowned when he checked Donnie's pack, but didn't say anything.

Donnie sat straight in the saddle, a defiant look on his face. Toby sidestepped and pulled at the bit.

Tory could see that Donnie was holding the reins too taut. The horse didn't like the constant pressure on his mouth. She slipped to Toby's side and tugged on the reins gently to remind the boy to loosen up without having to say something to embarrass him in front of the other campers. Donnie glared at her but relaxed his grip slightly.

As Sandy climbed onto Buckshot's back, Tory adjusted her pack and mounted up, too. Mayonnaise never flinched. She smoothed his creamy mane.

"Sandy looks great on Buckshot," she whispered to the paint. "They've both got fire and spunk." Catching Sandy's eye across the milling group, she gave her the A-OK sign. Sandy returned it, grinning broadly.

Brian waited until everyone was ready to go before he mounted his horse. He rode Bullet, a magnificent steel gray gelding that looked like something King Arthur would have ridden with the knights of the Round Table. The muscles rippled in his massive body as he pranced in circles, chomping at the bit.

"All right, group," Mike's voice rose above the clamor. "Brian and Sandy in front, Tory somewhere in the middle, and I'll bring up the rear with the buckboard."

A cloud of dust rose as excited campers struggled to rein their horses into two straight lines behind Sandy and Brian. Barney planted his pink hooves, refusing to budge. Tory reined Mayonnaise in close behind the stubborn albino. She could see tears welling up in Connie's eyes as she jabbed futilely at Barney's sides with her heels. Tory lifted the ends of her reins and smacked them down on Barney's rump. The horse jumped, startled, then plodded into line with no further resistance. Connie cast her a look of gratitude.

Tory reined Mayonnaise into line just behind Toby. She wanted to keep an eye on Donnie. A week would be plenty long enough for him to create some bad habits in a perfectly good horse. She had to admit that the boy and horse looked great together. Donnie's smoldering good looks matched Toby's flashy elegance perfectly.

"Great horse, Tory. Where'd you get him?" Todd and Merrilegs had pulled into line right beside her. "Doesn't look like old Walker, does he?"

Tory giggled. "No, I graduated. This is Mayonnaise. He's a 4-year-old I'm training in to be a trail horse." She shooed a fly from the gelding's left ear. "Nice, isn't he?"

Todd scrutinized the paint. "He is at that. Real nice." He watched Tory ride for awhile. "You're good with him," he said finally. "Mike knows what he's doing. You're going to have a crackerjack little trail horse when you get done."

"Thanks, Todd." Then she remembered her determination to give him a chance to talk if he needed to. "Hey, do you remember the night we sat by the campfire on the overnight pack trip?"

Todd grinned, "How could I forget? There I was sitting by the fire with a beautiful woman, stars twinkling overhead . . ." He batted his eyes playfully at Tory and laughed. "What about it?"

"You said you needed to talk, and I just wanted to let you know that I'd be glad to be a sounding board any time on the trip. Just say the word."

The boy looked away, suddenly quiet. "Ok. Maybe something will work out. Thanks."

Tory turned in the saddle to watch Big Jim for a while. He leaned into the harness, his massive shoulders pulling the loaded buckboard as effortlessly as if it had been a child's wagon. Mike sat straight in the seat, holding the reins like an English carriage driver. He whistled softly, keeping time with Jim's hoofbeats.

The horse's quiet, gentle, but very determined and hardworking nature impressed Tory. Just like Mike's. She admired them both.

"This is going to be a great week." Tory pulled a handful of leaves from a bush as they passed it, and threw them up in the air like confetti.

Sandy looked back just at that moment from her place at the front of the line. "No parties back there, Tory Butler," she called, pointing a finger at her in mock censure. The rest of the campers laughed and began making wisecracks. Over the din, Brian's clear voice rose, singing an old Irish ballad. Mike joined in, then one by one the campers picked up the tune. Tory closed her eyes to listen.

As the song faded, Tory realized with a start that she had no idea where they were going. She had been outside working with Mayonnaise when Mike and Brian finalized the route. Then she sighed. It didn't matter. Nothing mattered right now except the warm sun on her face and the gentle rocking of the horse beneath her. For this moment, right now, she was perfectly and utterly content.

CHAPTER NINE

Tory shifted in the saddle, trying to find a spot that wasn't sore. It seemed like days since the group had left Cool Springs Camp, but Tory knew it probably wasn't more than five or six hours ago. She pulled her canteen from its spot behind the cantle of her saddle and took a long drink. The water was warm, but she was thirsty.

The group had fallen silent.

Their voices are probably worn out from singing, Tory thought. Mike and Brian's repertoire of old camp tunes seemed inexhaustible.

Suddenly Brian called out, "Land, Ho! I see our camp, mates."

The campers came to life immediately. The horses sensed their excitement and picked up the pace. Brian hopped down from Bullet's back and led the horse to a corral fashioned from rope, tucked back in an oak grove. The soft ground under the towering old trees was perfect for setting up tents.

Tory pitched her tent on the south side of the grove, near those of several of the other girls. The boys took the north side. Mike disappeared into the woods behind the boy's camp with a camp shovel and a roll of toilet paper in his hand. She knew he was digging the boys latrine. When he reemerged, she hurried over.

"Our turn," she said, taking the little green shovel from Mike. "Please," she added, grinning.

"It's all yours, kiddo." Mike turned to unload supplies from the buckboard. He pulled a large piece of black plastic from a box and handed it to Tory. "There you go, cookie. That's your kitchen. What's for supper?"

Tory stared at the plastic, then back at Mike. "My kitchen?" She hadn't planned on having any kind of a kitchen on the trip. She and Sandy had divided the meals up for the week. Tory would organize suppers, and Sandy would do breakfasts. Sack lunches along the trail would suffice for the noon meals.

"Come on. I'll show you." Mike took the piece of plastic and within minutes fashioned a lean-to next to the stone fire pit he and Brian had built when they constructed the corral.

"Perfect. I love it!" Tory said when he finished.

After Mike brought a box of supplies and another of kitchen utensils, Tory organized them into a neat, orderly work space almost as functional as her mother's kitchen at home.

Her thoughts drifted back to the years she'd spent at home, helping her mom. It hadn't always seemed like fun then. She'd learned a lot, though, preparing meals for the family to reduce the burden on her mother who was working full-time to keep three children in church school. Making bread, pastries, and casseroles, canning fruits and vegetables . . . it all seemed simple now. And she knew the experience would serve her well in the days to come.

"Hi. Mike said we're the supper crew for tonight." Tory looked up to see Carol and Connie standing in front of her. Now that she saw them side by side, she was struck anew with the difference in appearance between the twins. She was careful, though, not to let her reaction show.

"All right!" Tory grabbed a couple of vegetable peelers and set the huge stewpot beside the fire. She handed each of the girls a peeler and a smaller bowl. "Vegetable stew and camp bread for supper. How does that sound?"

The girls nodded eagerly and fished through the vegetable box for potatoes, onions, and carrots. Tory helped them peel a mound of potatoes and carrots and cut them up into bite-sized chunks. She washed the vegetables with water Mike had carried along in 5-gallon containers, and threw them into the stewpot.

They saved the onions for last. Sitting cross-legged on the ground, Tory and the twins peeled the onions. Tears streamed down their faces as they sliced the onions for the stew.

"Hey, can I help?"

Tory peered through blurry eyes, trying to see who was speaking. It sounded like Brian's voice. She handed him an onion and her knife. "Sure. Have at it."

She got up and stumbled to one of the water jugs to douse her eyes. In a few minutes, her vision cleared. Then she walked back around the far side of the fire to the lean-to, avoiding the onion fumes.

Brian sat between the twins, tears streaming down his cheeks and dripping into the bowl of chopped onions in his lap. The trio sniffed and sputtered but kept chopping. Brian wiped a sleeve across his eyes.

"They say tears are healing," he said, solemnly. "We should all feel great after this session." The twins nodded, giggling.

Mike, Todd, and Donnie built a roaring fire and soon the pot of stew bubbled merrily, filling the camp with an inviting aroma. The other campers migrated toward the kitchen area like ants to a picnic. Tory pulled a box of baking mix from the lean-to and measured several cups of the white powder into a metal mixing bowl.

"OK, guys, watch carefully," she called out to the group. "This is camp bread, and you're going to make it."

She poured just enough water into the mix to make a sticky dough. Working it with her hands, she pulled a small handful of the dough from the bowl and rolled it between her palms like a child would roll modeling clay. Then she broke a long, thin branch from a nearby bush and wrapped the dough around the end. Finding the perfect bed of coals in the fire, she held the wad of dough over it, turning the stick constantly to allow all sides of the dough exposure to the heat.

The bread puffed up and turned a delicate golden brown as it baked. The campers watched hungrily as Tory pulled a piece of bread from the stick and started to pop it into her mouth. Then she stopped.

"Oops. Let's have the blessing. Then you can all make your own camp bread."

Tory glanced around, looking for Mike to have the prayer. He wasn't there. Brian sat near the fire watching Tory carefully, a bemused expression on his face. She felt her heart jump to her throat.

Finally he stood up.

"I'll say it," he said quietly. Before Tory could agree or disagree, Brian was praying. It was a simple, beautiful prayer. When he finished, she turned away, handing the bowl of dough to Connie.

"Here, dole it out, could you please? I want to go for a walk."

Wanting to be alone, Tory meandered down the trail, past the rope corral where the horses munched the hay Mike had tossed to them earlier in the evening. Frogs croaked in a nearby pond. Cicadas sang in the trees, a shrill chorus strangely soothing in its dissonance.

Brian's face loomed up in her mind. She resented his attraction to her. She tried to remember every girl she'd seen him with, reminding herself that he collected girls' hearts as if they were trophies for his showcase. But she couldn't shake the mental image of his eyes watching her. Of his sincere prayer. Of the sound of his voice as he sang. She walked on and on, until daylight thinned into twilight and she realized she might be caught in the dark if she didn't start back immediately.

As Tory approached the camp, she heard shrieks of laughter and Brian's voice booming above the others in a silly Mexican accent. She broke into the clearing and saw him, in a wide-brimmed sombrero, clowning for the campers who were crowded around the campfire. He was telling a story about a Mexican farmer and his donkey. Tory sat down in the circle next to Sandy and listened, laughing in spite of herself.

Sandy leaned over and whispered, "You'll have to admit, he is cute!" She poked Tory in the ribs and grinned. "Not as cute as Wally, of course, but nevertheless cute."

Tory scowled and turned away from Sandy. She positioned herself where she could watch the twins. A boy sat on each side of Carol, and she talked and laughed with both of them.

Connie perched on a log off by herself. Her arms wrapped around her knees, she watched her sister. Tory could feel her pain, even from this distance. She longed to wrap the girl in her arms and rock her, to soothe the hurt away, to reassure her that she was special just as she was. But she knew she couldn't. This battle was Connie's to fight. Tory prayed that she'd have an opportunity at some point during the week to say something to her.

CHAPTER
TEN

Morning arrived too soon. Tory rolled over in her sleeping bag and groaned. Every muscle in her body ached.

Sandy squatted by the campfire, flipping pancakes in the huge camp skillet as Tory staggered from her tent. "Rise and shine, friend of mine," she sang out.

"You're disgustingly cheerful for such an ungodly hour," Tory complained, but she had to admit the pancakes smelled awfully good. A gnawing sensation in her stomach reminded her that she hadn't eaten since lunchtime yesterday. She perched on a rock beside Sandy like a hungry baby bird waiting to be fed.

Sandy held a pancake out to her. "Get a plate, Tory, and I'll give you this culinary masterpiece." Motioning toward the lean-to, she said, "They're over there with the toppings. On the counter by the sink." She snickered at her own joke.

Tory found the plates on a board placed on the ground beside a 5-gallon water container. Blueberry pie filling, syrup, jam, and butter had been artistically arranged next to the forks and cups.

Sandy sniffed. "Just because we're camping is no reason to be uncivilized." She lifted her pert nose in a pose of mock snobbery.

"OK, Emily Post." Tory held her plate out. "Just give me a pancake, please. We can discuss etiquette later." She looked up. Campers scurried around, busily packing up tents and bedding.

"Has everyone else eaten?" she gulped.

"Yes, ma'am." Sandy tossed another pancake onto Tory's plate. "Mike says it's a long, hot ride today . . . says we should 'head 'em up and move 'em out as soon as possible,' to quote the man!"

Tory inhaled the pancakes and then bowed to Sandy. "My compliments to the chef," she said solemnly before hurrying to her tent to pack up.

She pulled the stakes from her tent and folded it into a compact roll. Hearing footsteps behind her, she looked up to see Todd holding Mayonnaise's reins in one hand and Merrilegs' in the other. Both horses were groomed and saddled. Todd had already tied his pack neatly to the back of his saddle. He grinned at her look of surprise. "Thought you could use a little help this morning." After tying Mayonnaise's reins to a nearby tree branch, he hopped up onto Merrilegs' back.

"Thanks!" Tory stared at him as he rode back to the boys' side of the grove, then shook her head in amazement.

Mike hadn't exaggerated about the ride being long and hot that day. Tory rode in the very back of the line for a while, watching for stragglers. Dust clouds billowed behind the wagon and puffed up with each hoofstep.

She realized with annoyance that Brian was riding right in her line of vision. After he took his shirt off and tied it to his saddle, Tory watched his back, tanned and muscular, bobbing along on Bullet's back. She wondered if he wished Jan were along instead of her.

"Tory, do you have a minute?" Todd had pulled Merrilegs back to get into step with Mayonnaise.

"Sure." She sensed that he had something in mind. She slowed Mayonnaise's pace and gave Todd her full attention. "What's up?"

"I, er, well . . ." He squirmed uncomfortably in the saddle, obviously struggling for the right words.

A sudden gust of wind whipped down the line of riders, blowing small twigs and leaves into the air. Tory glanced at the sky and gasped. Menacing clouds piled thick and dark in the east. The horses began to prance nervously.

"Stay together," Mike shouted above the wind. "Pick up the pace, Brian. Let's try to make it to the campsite before this storm breaks."

A clap of thunder rolled across the sky. Tory watched helplessly as Midnight bolted from the line with Carol hanging on like a monkey on an organ grinder's back. Quickly Brian turned Bullet sideways in their path and reached out to grab Midnight's reins before he could get past.

Urging Mayonnaise into a canter, Tory hurried to Carol's side. The girl sat huddled on Midnight's back, crying softly and shaking all over. Tory pulled Mayonnaise up closer beside Midnight and wrapped her arms around the frightened girl. "It's OK, Carol.

I'm here. I'll stay beside you until we get to camp."
Just then Tory looked up and saw Brian watching her.
He flashed her a smile.

"Thanks, Tory," he said.

She smiled back. "Thank *you*. You reacted
quickly. No telling where Midnight would be right
now if you hadn't stopped him."

Brian shrugged and wheeled Bullet around in the
path. He pointed to the glowering sky. "We'd better
all hustle if we don't want to get drenched."

The horses were happy to pick up their speed.
They seemed just as eager as the humans to find shel-
ter before the storm broke. The group arrived at the
campsite just in time to set up the tents and crawl in
before huge drops of rain began pelting down.

The campers huddled miserably in their tents,
munching granola bars and fruit, and watching lightening dance and flash across the sky. Tory had always been amazed at the ferocity of a Florida
electrical storm, and this one was no exception.

From where she sat in her tent, she could see the
rope corral Mike and Brian had hastily constructed.
The horses hunkered together in the deluge, rain
streaming down their flanks and dripping from their
muzzles. Tory felt sorry for them. It didn't seem fair
that she got to sit in a dry tent while they had to re-
main out in the storm.

A two-legged figure appeared among the horses,
collar turned up against the storm. He moved from
horse to horse, apparently reassuring each one and
checking for problems. A second figure joined him.
The two turned toward the tents as they inspected the

corral to make sure it was intact, and Tory could see that they were Mike and Brian.

She snuggled contentedly down in her sleeping bag. It comforted her to know that no matter what happened, she could trust the wranglers to take care of all of them—horses, campers, and staff alike. It was a good feeling.

Raindrops beat a drum roll on the rain fly of Tory's tent. Through the din, she thought she heard a whimpering sound, like a lonely puppy crying. Holding her breath, she listened carefully. The sound rose and fell. It seemed to be coming from the tent next to hers.

Tory crawled out into the rain, shivering as huge cold drops splatted on the back of her neck. She positioned herself just outside the neighboring tent and listened again. This time she heard muffled sobs, as if someone were crying into a pillow. Clearing her throat, she called softly, "Are you OK in there? It's Tory." The sobs stopped immediately, and Connie's tear-streaked face appeared in the tent opening.

"I'm sorry," she said, a stricken look in her eyes. "I didn't think anyone would hear me over the storm."

"Hearing you or not isn't the point," Tory said, approaching the tent. She shook the rain from her hair. "May I come in?"

"S-sure." Connie scooted aside and made room for her. Tory wrapped the end of Connie's sleeping bag around her shoulders to keep warm, then turned to the girl, who looked away, quickly wiping her face.

"You don't have to be embarrassed about your tears, Connie," Tory said quietly. "They're something

God gave us to help get us through hard times. What I'm more concerned about right now is why you're hurting so much. Do you want to talk about it?"

Connie sniffled and stared at her fingernails. Finally she looked up, her eyes brimming with pain.

"You have no idea how hard it is to have a beautiful sister and always come up short," she said miserably. "I'm sure she's not afraid of this horrid storm. Probably she's sitting in somebody's tent playing Rook and having a great time, while I lay here with my pillow over my head."

Tory sat quietly, listening, not wanting to interrupt. She reached over and worked the muscles of Connie's neck with her thumbs as the girl talked.

"We both looked forward to this trip so much. It's all we talked about for months. Now all I can think about is going home." Tears streamed down her face and strands of curly blond hair lay damp against her temples.

"I hate this rain, I hate the horse I'm riding. I hate being jealous of my sister. And I hate myself for being such a loser.

"Bursting into tears, she buried her face in Tory's shoulder. Tory wrapped her arms around the girl and rocked her gently back and forth, holding her until the tears were spent.

"Do you mind if I share something with you?" Tory finally asked. Connie shook her head.

"I was feeling pretty bad myself a couple weeks ago. Bad enough that I was ready to quit and go home, too."

The girl sat up and stared at her in the dim tent.

"You wanted to quit?"

"Yes." Tory sighed. "Things looked pretty bleak to me. A girl much prettier then I am wanted this position, and I was sure she'd get it because of her looks and popularity.

"To top it all off, Mike gave me a stubborn old nag that wouldn't do a thing I wanted him to."

"Like Barney," Connie exclaimed. "Why would he do that?"

Tory laughed. "Did you ever hear the old saying, 'Adversity strengthens the character'? Well, I think Mike operates under some variation of that theme. I can guarantee you one thing, though. It's no accident that he gave you Barney. And if you'll give it a chance, something good will come of it."

"I think I'd rather be beautiful than have a strong character," Connie muttered.

Tory smiled. "You can have both, you know."

The girl shook her head. "How? Plastic surgery?"

"No-o-o," Tory said slowly. "Stop and think. Who do you know that's beautiful? Really beautiful? Not just perfect features. They sag and wrinkle in a few years anyway."

A thoughtful expression on her face, Connie sat up even straighter. "My mom. She's great. And my pastor's wife."

"OK. Tell me why they're pretty."

Connie's face puckered into a frown of concentration. "They're just good," she blurted out finally. "And kind. They just kind of light up from the inside."

Tory nodded. "Serenity, integrity, and unconditional love. The three keys to unfading beauty. They don't have much to do with the face you're born with, do they?"

The girl mulled the idea over, then shook her head, grinning. "I guess not."

The wind had died down, and Tory could see the sun peeking through the clouds. The storm had passed. Raindrops glistened on the tree leaves, and the horses milled restlessly in the corral, ready for their supper. Tory pulled the tent flap back to climb out, then turned back to Connie. "I'd like to pass along some words of wisdom that a friend shared with me a few weeks ago, if you want to hear them." The girl nodded. "'You are a unique and valuable child of God with a lot to offer in life.' Repeat that to yourself at least three times a day for a month. Doctor's orders."

Connie laughed and saluted. "Yes, ma'am." Her blue eyes sparkled.

Sandy stood outside her tent as Tory emerged, a concerned expression on her face. "I thought I heard someone crying earlier. Is Connie OK?"

"Yep, I think she's going to be just fine." She picked a daisy from a clump near the campsite and poked her head back into Connie's tent. "Here's something to remind you of what of what we talked about." She handed the girl the flower and gave her a quick hug. "Don't forget now."

Connie's blue eyes sparkled. "I won't. I promise."

Tory crawled back out of Connie's tent and smiled at Sandy's quizzical expression. "It's a long story. I'll tell you later," Tory whispered and held a finger to her lips. "Let's just say Connie's in the process of finding herself."

"I'll take your word for it." Sandy grinned and shrugged. She held up two metal feed buckets. "Mike wants us to feed the horses." She threw one of the buckets to Tory. "I'll beat you to the buckboard."

The girls raced across the wet grass, arriving at the buckboard at exactly the same moment. They fell to the ground, gasping for breath.

"I won," Tory croaked. "I touched the buckboard first."

Panting, Sandy shook her head. "Nope. I won, and I'm right here by the feed bag."

Brian stepped from behind the buckboard, carrying two bucketfuls of grain. "Actually, neither of you won. I beat you both," he snickered.

Tory shook her head. "There has to be a lesson in this somewhere, but I'm not sure it's something I want to know."

Brian grinned and headed for the corral. "Don't think too hard," he called over his shoulder. "You might blow a fuse."

Tory made a face at him and turned to Sandy. "What a brat," she said, smiling.

Sandy looked up at her, an amused expression on her face. "Somehow you don't sound very sincere. Is your opinion of Don Juan changing?"

Tory blushed and stared at her feet. "Maybe." She pushed a twig around on the ground with the toe of her shoe. "He seems pretty nice, now that I've gotten to know him."

Standing and brushing the sand from her jeans, Sandy said, "I hear violins playing." She cupped her hand over her ear and laughed.

Tory filled her bucket with grain and turned away, frowning. "I think *you're* tone-deaf, and I have work to do."

"It's 'Unchained Melody,'" Sandy called after her. Tory could hear her laughing all the way to the corral.

CHAPTER ELEVEN

T he morning air felt fresh and clean after the storm. Tory was the first one up. She hated to pack a wet tent, but knew she would have no time to dry it before they headed out on the trail. According to Mike, today would be the longest stretch of the trip.

She shook as much moisture off the fabric as she could, then rolled the tent carefully and tucked it into her pack. She moved her dry clothes to a spot where they wouldn't touch the tent.

"I'm not putting that wet stuff in my pack," a boy's voice complained. Tory turned to see Donnie standing beside his soaked gear, a scowl on his face.

Calmly Mike walked over to Donnie's campsite. "We're heading out in 20 minutes. Pack it," he said quietly, then turned and left. Donnie poked at the soggy mass, muttering angrily, but made no real attempt to pack it.

Tory shook her head. The boy was in a bad mood today. Earlier she'd had to stop him from teasing a couple of girls. He didn't seem to know when to quit. Hurrying to the corral to get Mayonnaise, she realized that she'd be doing well just to get him saddled and her own pack secured before they started.

When she returned a few minutes later, Donnie stood beside Toby, his pack thrown haphazardly behind the saddle. She tethered Mayonnaise to a bush and turned to the boy.

"Would you like some help tying that pack on, Donnie? I'm not sure it'll take a long day on the trail like that."

The boy gave her a look of disdain. "No. I can tie it myself. I don't need your help."

With a shrug she went back to securing her own pack.

The group moved out, Brian and Sandy in the lead, Tory and Mike bringing up the rear. The horses seemed eager to hit the trail. The cool clean air brought out their frisky side. Even Barney pranced along, head up and ears erect to catch every sound along the path. Tory smiled to herself as she watched Connie sitting tall in the saddle, an eager expression on her face.

An armadillo waddled across the path like a little armored tank. The campers stopped and crowded their horses in close to see the odd creature. Suddenly Sandy squealed. "Look. *Babies!*"

Half a dozen tiny pink replicas of the mother armadillo scurried across the path and disappeared into the palmetto thicket. Everyone laughed and chattered excitedly about the encounter.

Brian motioned for the line of riders to reform, and everyone headed down the trail again. Tory watched Donnie, several horses ahead of her, squirming in his saddle, fumbling with his pack every few minutes. She could tell by its skewed position at the back of his saddle that it was just a matter of time until it would be on the ground. She glanced over at Mike and noticed that he was watching Donnie, too.

Suddenly Donnie reined Toby to a stop and turned to rearrange his pack. Barney, the notorious tailgater, plowed into Toby's hindquarters. With a squeal, Toby kicked up his heels and the pack went flying. Its contents spewed in every direction.

Donnie jumped to the ground, his face livid. "Stop the line!" he shouted. "I lost my pack."

Brian rode back to see what the problem was. Donnie stomped back and forth, picking up his scattered clothing. When Brian looked at Mike, the older wrangler shook his head and motioned for Brian to keep moving. Rejoining Sandy in the front of the line, Brian shouted, "Come on. Let's go."

Donnie stood beside the path and stared in disbelief at Mike, then at Brian, finally jerking Toby to the side of the trail.

Mike sat calmly in the buckboard as he approached the furious boy. He gazed straight ahead until he was close enough to lean over and whisper to the boy without the other campers overhearing. Tory couldn't make out all the words but she heard Mike say something about consequences and accepting responsibility.

As the group rounded a bend in the trail, Tory glanced back. Behind them Donnie sat in the path with his chin in his hands, his pack piled in disarray beside him. Toby munched contentedly on a clump of clover, apparently not the least bit worried about being left behind.

The day wore on, hot and sultry. Tory caught glimpses of Donnie periodically throughout the day, following at a distance, too proud to rejoin the group. The boy looked lonely. One time, when he ventured close enough, Tory motioned for him to join them. He turned his head away and pulled his horse to a halt until the line had moved out of sight.

She sighed to herself. It seemed like such a hard lesson for Donnie. While she acknowledged the wisdom in Mike's decision, she still hated to see the boy so miserable.

The dust billowed up from the horses' hooves until the air seemed thick enough to chew. Tory coughed and rubbed her eyes. Grains of sand clung to them.

Mike waved to her and called, "Do this." Then she watched him pour water over his red handkerchief and tie it over his nose and mouth. She hesitated, not sure she wanted to deplete her precious water supply. Finally she pulled the handkerchief from her neck and doused it down.

The wet handkerchief made an incredible difference. Suddenly she could breathe again. The cool, damp air soothed her throat and lungs. She nodded and waved to Mike.

The horses' heads drooped lower and lower. Tory could tell they were tired and thirsty too. Every step Mayonnaise took sent shock waves up her spine, and the handkerchief began drying almost as soon as she dampened it. Tory wondered how much longer she would be able to endure the heat.

A restless undercurrent rippled through the line

of campers.

"I'm thirsty. Can I have a drink of your water?"

"No. Mine's all gone."

"How much longer? I can't take much more of this!"

"Why is it so hot? My brains are baking."

"I want to go swimming. *Now!*"

"My horse is about ready to drop dead under me."

Tory checked her canteen and realized with horror that she had one swallow of water left. She moistened her dry lips and stood up in the saddle, hoping to see the campsite ahead. Heat waves danced in the trail, looking for all the world like cool puddles of water.

Closing her eyes, she imagined herself lost in the desert on her camel, searching for a spring to refill her goatskin water bottle. A mirage floated in the distance, palm trees waving invitingly. She urged her camel on, the scent of dates and coconuts wafting in the breeze. The mirage moved away as she approached. Her mouth felt like it was stuffed with cotton and her eyes burned. How long could she go on like this before she died of thirst . . . ?

"Tory, wake up!"

She jerked her eyes open. Todd plodded along beside her on Merrilegs. Even the indefatigable little welsh was obviously dragging his hooves.

"I wasn't asleep. I was fantasizing. I'm glad you interrupted me. I was almost dead."

"Well, I think *I'm* going to be dead soon if I don't get a drink. My water's gone." He turned his canteen upside down to illustrate his point. "Do you have any left?"

She offered hers. "Enough to wet your lips, that's all. But go ahead. Then we can all die of thirst together."

Todd shook his head and pushed her canteen back. "I can't take your last swallow of water. Surely it won't be too much farther."

The clear notes of "Amazing Grace" rose suddenly above everyone's muttering. Brian's rich baritone voice carried over the scrub like a church bell.

Tory and Todd looked at each other and shrugged, joining in the chorus. Soon the campers were all singing. "When the Roll Is Called Up Yonder" followed, then "I Will Make You Fishers of Men." Even the horses came alive, their ears perking up to catch the sound of their singing riders.

Mike joined in, singing harmony.

Tory almost forgot her thirst as the air rang with old hymns, gospel favorites, campfire songs, and silly ditties she'd never heard before. She laughed and sang until she was hoarse. Then she rode along quietly beside Todd, observing Mike and Brian's interaction with the campers.

"They just changed everyone's whole entire mood," Tory whispered.

Todd grinned. "The power of a positive attitude. Singing will do it every time. I've seen them do this many times before."

Tory shook her head. "It's amazing." She fell silent again and just watched Brian. His head thrown back, he sang with total abandon.

Maybe, Tory thought, *just maybe there's more to this guy than I gave him credit for.*

CHAPTER TWELVE

ory felt her thirst resurfacing. The singing had distracted her for a while but now her parched throat screamed for water. With a groan she lay her head against Mayonnaise's mane. "I'm dying. This is it. Just bury me along the trail."

Todd laughed and mopped his face with an old T-shirt. "It can't be much farther. The horses are picking up their pace." He pointed at Mayonnaise's muzzle. "Watch his nostrils flaring, Tory. He smells water!"

Suddenly the path broke out into a clearing. A magnificent spring, larger even than the one back at camp, sparkled in the sunlight. Crystal clear with a deep blue swimming hole and moss-draped oaks lining its banks, the spring beckoned the thirsty travelers.

Brian let out a war whoop and kicked Bullet into a dead run, several of the boys hot on his heels. They splashed into the spring, the horses snorting and pawing, gulping mouthfuls of the cool water.

Tory slipped from Mayonnaise's back and led him to the edge of the spring. After tying his reins to the saddle horn, leaving him plenty of slack to move his head up and down, she dove into the water, clothes and all.

She swam with the group for an hour before she started to shiver. It felt wonderful to be cold after the long hot ride. She climbed out onto the bank and lay on her back in the sun, staring up at the treetops and listening to the squirrels scolding each other.

Mayonnaise grazed contentedly in the meadow beside the spring with the other horses. His reins had loosened from the saddle horn and fallen to the ground, but he kept his head tilted slightly to the side as he walked to avoid stepping on them.

"You smartie, you," Tory called when she spotted what he was doing. Jumping up, she ran to Mayonnaise and pulled the bridle off to allow him more freedom to move around. Then she loosened the cinch and took off his saddle, tossing it over a nearby log. Mayonnaise shook all over, then resumed his grazing.

Mike and Brian, their clothes still dripping, constructed a corral. Sandy and Tory helped haze the horses into the enclosure while Mike doled out buckets of grain to the hungry herd. As usual when being fed, the horses bit and kicked each other until they reestablished a satisfactory pecking order. Barney stood belligerently over his bucket, ears pinned flat against his head, daring anyone to challenge his right to feed there.

"You hard-headed old geezer," Tory laughed, turning to help Mike unload the buckboard. The wrangler nodded and grinned.

"He's persistent, isn't he? Great quality."

Tory stopped and stared at Mike. He actually *ad-*

mired the horse. She had never thought of his obstinence as being praiseworthy. But when she pictured Connie and all the personal obstacles she faced, suddenly it all made sense. Mike had assigned Connie to Barney to teach her to be persistent! She smiled to herself as she unloaded the supper box. Leave it to Mike.

Hotdogs, marshmallows, and spring-chilled watermelon made up the fare. Tory sent the campers scurrying to find roasting sticks while Mike and Brian built a roaring bonfire. The fire sent showers of sparks like miniature meteors into the air.

Tory sat on a log and dangled a hot dog over some coals. Connie sidled up to her and poked a stick with three marshmallows on the end into the spot next to Tory's. She left the marshmallows close to the coals until they burst into flame, then quickly blew the fire out. Pulling the charred gooey mass from the end of her stick, she popped it into her mouth.

"M-m-m," Connie closed her eyes in ecstasy. "I *love* burnt marshmallows."

Tory shuddered. The sickeningly sweet puffs of sugar were bad enough without being torched. Thankfully she gazed at her golden brown hot dog.

Connie slipped her arm shyly through her's, sat quietly for a moment, then sighed.

"This is so wonderful. I'm glad I stayed. I wouldn't have missed this for the world." She grinned. "You know, Tory, I was so busy focusing on how I thought everyone else was better than me, that I wasn't paying any attention to the ways *I'm* special. I've thought about it a lot since we talked. Thanks."

"You're welcome." Tory squeezed the girl's hand.

As she pulled her hot dog from the fire and stood to get a bun from the makeshift serving table on the tailgate of the buckboard, she saw a figure moving on the other side of the spring. Darkness had fallen and she couldn't tell who it was in the gathering shadows.

When she approached closer she saw Donnie standing near the buckboard, a half-eaten slice of watermelon in his hand and red juice dripping from his chin. He sucked in his breath to spit the watermelon seed as far as he could. Tory was surprised to see him there. He had kept his distance from any of the staff members since they'd arrived at camp, still sulking over being left behind that morning.

"Hi, Donnie. How's the melon?" She flashed him a smile, hoping to break the ice.

"OK," he muttered and turned away.

Sighing heavily, she reached for the ketchup. Donnie sure seemed to have a chip on his shoulder.

Munching her hot dog, she strolled along the path around the spring. Crickets chirped and the moon's reflection rippled on the silent surface of the water. Tory found a log overhanging the spring and sat down to absorb the wonder of the moment.

A movement at the other end of the spring caught her eye. She stiffened then relaxed as Brian meandered into the moonlight. Tory caught her breath. Had he seen her sitting there? She wasn't sure. The log was tucked back under a huge tree and partially obscured by branches.

Suddenly he turned and walked straight toward the spot where she sat. Just then Todd stepped out of the shadows. "Hi, Tory. Do you mind if I sit here with you for a while?"

Tory patted the log beside her. "Of course not. Have a seat."

Todd sank down beside Tory. She glanced up at his face and saw tears brimming in his eyes.

"I just need to talk to somebody. I've had something on my mind for a while, and it's driving me nuts."

He was about to continue when Brian reached the log.

"Hey, you two. What do you think of the view from here?" Brian took a deep breath and sighed contentedly. "Paradise, isn't it?"

Tory leaned back out of Todd's field of vision and tried to motion to Brian to go away, but Brian just stared at her without comprehending. She tried some sign language she'd learned in academy, but he just shook his head.

Todd looked at Brian then back at Tory. Jumping to his feet, he offered his place to Brian.

"I've got to go, anyway. You two talk." He sprinted off down the path before Tory could protest.

She groaned. "Something is bothering him and he was just about to tell me what it is," she told Brian.

He stared at the boy's retreating figure, a stricken look on his face. "I'm sorry, Tory. I didn't mean to interrupt."

She shook her head. "It's OK. There's no way you could have known. There'll be other opportunities. I just hope he's OK."

"Me, too." Brian sat down on the log beside her. Pulling a spear of grass from a clump behind the log, he chewed on the end of it. "I came to see if you wanted to take a walk. The moon is so bright tonight it's almost like walking in daylight."

Tory felt her heart start pounding. Her palms were clammy and cold. Suddenly there was nothing she wanted more in the world than to walk with him. But just then a mental image of Jan hanging on his arm and whispering in his ear flashed into her mind. She shook her head.

"No," she said curtly. "I really need to get to bed. It's been a long day. Thanks, anyway."

As she rounded a bend in the path she glanced back to see him staring after her, a bewildered expression on his face. She clenched her teeth as she strode back to camp.

"Brian Winters," she muttered. "This is one girl who is not going to fall for you."

CHAPTER THIRTEEN

By morning the campfire had burned down to a mammoth bed of coals. Some of the boys had obviously fed it throughout the night. Tory stood by the glowing embers, warming her hands. The air still had a nip to it, and the heat from the coals felt good.

"Hey, Tory," Mike called. "Let's bake some potatoes in that coal bed!"

Tory turned in surprise. "How can we do that? Don't we have to pack up and move on?"

Mike grinned and pulled a wooden crate filled with potatoes, onions, and carrots from the buckboard.

"Naw. Let's just stay here and rest today." When he winked at Brian she realized that they had already planned another day at the site.

As Sandy walked up from the spring, Mike tossed her a roll of aluminum foil.

"Gather 'round, ladies and gents." Mike whistled for the campers. "We will now have a demonstration of the ultimate in camp cookery." He showed Sandy how to measure off sections of the tin foil and motioned to Tory to help him wrap the vegetables snugly.

The campers watched Brian rake the coals to

the side of the campfire pit and toss the shiny mounds into the bed. Then he raked the coals back over the vegetables.

"There." Brian brushed his hands together in satisfaction. "In a few hours we'll have the world's best meal. And in the meantime, who wants to take a bareback ride to the river?"

The campers clapped their hands and ran for the corral, whooping with delight. The river lay a mile to the east of the spring. The trail through the palmettos was narrow and overgrown. Tory followed the others, determined not to be left behind.

Brian was already heading down the trail at a canter on Bullet's muscular back when Tory led Mayonnaise out of the corral. Donnie flashed by on Toby with Todd and Merrilegs close behind.

"Come on, slow poke," Todd called. Tory threw her leg over Mayonnaise's back and grabbed a handful of his coarse mane to keep her balance. She kicked the gelding into a gallop to catch up with the others, wincing as the sharp palmetto stalks scratched her legs. Then she held her legs as high as she could to keep them above the level of the brush.

The scrub echoed with Brian and Donnie's Indian war cries as they crashed through the brush at a dead run. Tory's eyes blurred with tears and Mayonnaise's mane whipped her face as he ran.

Without warning, the trail broke out into a clearing. The coffee-colored river snaked lazily by. Cypress trees towered over its banks, their knobby knees protruding from the water's edge. Donnie and Brian were already out in the current, swimming

Toby and Bullet upstream. Then Donnie stood on Toby's back and waved to the others on the bank.

Tory sat on Mayonnaise and loosened the reins so he could drink the dark water. As she watched Donnie's bravado, she couldn't help but compare it to Todd's silence.

"I know they're both hurting," she whispered to Mayonnaise. She sighed. "But people are like horses. Each has his own personality and temperament. And some people find it really hard to ask for help."

After Tory slipped from Mayonnaise's back and led him to a patch of grass to graze, she sat on the river bank to watch the horses swim. Todd and Merrilegs had joined the others in the current.

"Father," Tory prayed, "I'd love to help Todd and Donnie if I can. Please give me the wisdom and the opportunity to reach out to each of them somehow."

Two hours later, the group straggled back into camp, soaked and muddy. The aroma of baked vegetables filled the air. Mike had already raked the coals back and piled the foil-covered veggies beside the campfire pit. Now he sat on the buckboard tailgate, his plate piled with onions, carrots, and potatoes.

"You almost missed out," Mike teased. "I could eat them all myself."

Pulling a round shape from the pile, Tory peeled back the ash-covered foil to reveal an onion. She plunked it onto her plate and broke it open, breathing the savory steam that billowed from the onion's insides.

"Try this, Tory." Mike pushed a tub of margarine and a lemon slice toward Tory. "It'll transform that

109

onion into a culinary delight."

Tory spread the onion with margarine, then squeezed lemon juice into the layers. Her mouth watered as the tangy lemon smell filled her nostrils. She took a mouthful and closed her eyes. The onion's incredibly rich flavor was like nothing she'd ever tasted. "Mmm," she sighed, "that is food for the gods."

As Brian sat on the grass near the fire pit, Donnie squatted nearby, obviously watching every move he made and trying to imitate him without being obvious. Clearly the boy admired Brian and looked up to him as a role model. Tory smiled to herself.

Friday dawned bright and clear. The trail ride to the next camping area was short. By noon, the campers were pitching their tents for Sabbath. Tory and Sandy organized the black plastic kitchen. They worked with Todd and another boy to fix a supper of beans and rice.

The new campsite bordered another beautiful, though smaller, spring. As the sun set, Mike assembled the staff and campers on a grassy slope that overlooked the water. A sense of tranquility settled over the camp. Tory smiled to herself. Sabbath was always such a treat.

Mike stood in front of the group and talked about the special opportunities the week had presented so far. He pointed out how even the simplest experience can teach a valuable spiritual lesson.

"Would anyone like to share something you learned this week?" He paused, giving the group a chance to think.

Connie raised her hand shyly.

"I learned something from the storm." She smiled at Tory. "I was terrified by the lightening, miserable, discouraged, and ready to go home. When I prayed for help, Tory came just a few minutes later to talk to me. I learned that God can even hear me through a storm."

Todd spoke next.

"I thought it would be next to impossible for Merrilegs to keep up with the bigger horses this week because his legs are so much shorter." He laughed and shook his head. "I was dead wrong. The other horses had to work to keep with *him*. What that little guy lacks in size, he makes up for in spirit. He has more spunk than any horse I've ever known. I guess I learned that it's not how tall you are that counts—it's how much you pour of yourself into everything you do."

Several of the campers nodded in agreement. Sandy stood.

"This week has been an incredible experience for me." She looked around at the group. "You've all become like family. Together we've sang and prayed and fussed and complained and hoped and dreamed. I learned that sharing experiences makes them much more precious. And that even those experiences that seemed negative at the time make great stories to tell later."

Brian rose to his feet just as she sat down. He tweaked the corner of his black mustache. "I saw a lot of teamwork this week. You helped each other with your packs, you joined together to fix great meals, you worked with your horses. I learned how much easier life is for everybody when there's a spirit of cooperation."

Tory glanced at Donnie sitting just behind and to her right. He stared at his shoes as he listened to the others. She wondered what was going through his mind. Then, slowly, he rose to his feet.

"I've learned something from some of you here," he said, kicking a clump of grass with his toe. Then he looked straight at Mike and Brian. "It didn't matter how rotten I felt, or how much I didn't want to do what you asked me to, you guys were patient. You never got mad or yelled at me. You let me learn my own way even if you disagreed. I want to be just like you."

His cheeks scarlet, Donnie sat down quickly. Brian and Mike stared at each other in surprise. Mike was the first to regain his composure. "OK, group, I have something for each of you." He held up a paper bag and pulled out a candle. "Each of you take a candle, please. Tory, Sandy, Brian, and I will be holding burning candles. Light your candle from one of ours, then form small groups to share with each other some of the special highlights of the trip so far."

Tory stood next to Sandy, her candle flame flickering in the gathering darkness. One by one the campers lit their candles and settled themselves in different spots around the spring. The candles glowed like huge fireflies against the dark water.

Suddenly splashes and screams jerked Tory's attention to a group of girls who had been sitting on the beach. Tory raced to the scene. The girls began shrieking and running back and forth, chattering so fast she couldn't understand a word they said.

Carol's limp body lay on the sand, hair and

clothes dripping wet.

"She was drowning," one of the girls sobbed. "We saved her."

Tory bent over Carol, feeling for a pulse. It was strong. She held her cheek close to Carol's mouth and nose and felt air moving in and out, then watched the girl's chest rise and fall with each breath she took.

"Connie, go get Mike," Tory ordered. "Have him call an ambulance." Just then Carol opened her eyes and sat up.

"Please don't call Mike," she begged. "I don't need an ambulance. Honest, I don't. I slipped and fell into the shallow water. I'm fine."

Tory helped the girl to her tent and found some dry clothes for her. With Carol snug and warm again, Tory sat Indian-style beside her and looked her straight in the eye.

"OK, Carol. Come clean," she said firmly. "What happened down there? Why did you want everybody to think you were drowning?"

The girl hung her head and was silent for a long time.

"I'm sorry," she said finally. "I guess I did it to get attention."

"So you thought staging a drowning would get you the kind of attention you want?"

"No, er, I guess not." Carol looked almost frightened. "It's just that Connie seems so confident lately. I don't know how to . . ."

Tory put her arm around Carol's shoulder and suddenly understood. "So you're afraid she's catching up with you?"

Carol nodded miserably.

"What if I told you Connie's not even on the same path you are so there's no chance of her ever catching up with you?" She could tell that the girl was listening carefully. "Connie could be the best Connie that it's possible for her to be and never, ever be Carol, even for a second. And you could be the best Carol and never be Connie at all." Tory squeezed the girl's shoulder. "It's a full time job just being Carol, isn't it?"

A sheepish grin on her face, Carol nodded. "I guess I've been wasting a lot of energy competing with my sister. I think I need to have a talk with her." Carol gave Tory a quick hug and disappeared into the night.

As she walked back from Carol's tent, Tory saw two figures coming up the path. They drew closer and she recognized Mike and Brian. "Hey, you guys. I think we made some progress with the twins tonight." Briefly she shared the experience she'd had with Carol.

Mike grinned. "Good work, Tory. Now would you like to hear what happened to Brian?"

Tory nodded eagerly. "Sure!"

Brian shook his head in amazement. "I guess I'm still in shock. Donnie joined our discussion group tonight and admitted to the others how lost and empty he felt. He asked me right there how to surrender his life to Christ, so I told him." A look of awe on his face, Brian smiled. "I led the group in commitment prayer, and he surrendered his life to God right there."

Tory sent up a quick "thank you" that at least part of her prayer had been answered. Now if she could just talk to Todd . . .

CHAPTER FOURTEEN

Oatmeal bubbled in the stewpot over the fire. Tory stood by the buckboard and doled out sweet rolls, boiled eggs, and fruit saved special for Sabbath breakfast.

Donnie held back to be last through line. He reached for the sweet roll Tory offered, then paused. "Can I ask you something?"

"Sure." Tory hopped up on the tailgate of the buckboard. She tossed an egg in the air and Donnie caught it, laughing.

"I was just wondering what this Sabbath stuff is. Friday night sundown . . . Sabbath breakfast. I don't know what everyone is talking about."

Realizing that the boy's family must not be church members, Tory took a deep breath. "Oh, I guess it never was explained, was it? I can just tell you what it means to me."

"OK." Donnie sat down beside her. "Tell me."

"The word Sabbath just means 'rest.' It's the one day of the week that we get to set aside for getting our spiritual batteries recharged. God said to do it in the fourth commandment because He knew a lot of us would be workaholics and run ourselves into the ground."

Donnie frowned. "So you just sit around and do nothing on Sabbath? Sounds pretty boring to me."

She laughed. "Nope. That's not how I spend it. I do whatever brings me closer to God." She waved an arm toward the spring. "Being out like this does it better than anything I know. Sabbath is like a date with God. I do things that don't distract me from our relationship during that special time. It's great."

Slowly Donnie nodded. "Guess it makes sense to me. A little weird, but it does make sense." He jumped down from the wagon. "Thanks for explaining it."

"Sure. No problem." Tory marveled at the change in him. The brittle hostility was gone.

Breakfast over, Mike called the group to sit in a ring on the grass. Tory glanced around the circle. The girls who had become hysterical the night before at Carol's faked drowning now sported sheepish grins. Tory noticed that Carol and Connie were sitting beside each other for the first time on the pack trip.

Tory sat down beside Todd as Mike began to speak. "I just wanted to take a few minutes to share some of the things I've observed about you guys this week. Since this is the last day of the pack trip, I might not have another chance."

Mike looked around the circle and began to describe the special character strengths of each person. He focused on Donnie's quick wit, his leadership skills, and his potential as a great worker. Next he encouraged each of the twins to develop their own unique qualities. Todd he praised for his sensitive nature and perceptiveness. Tory watched the boy out of the corner of her eye. He sat crosslegged in the grass staring at the ground.

After he'd spoken about everyone else in the group, Mike grinned and waved an arm in Tory's direction. "Now there's a real woman." She felt her face grow hot, but Mike went on to describe her sense of responsibility and dependability. "You girls would do well to use her as a role model."

Tory looked up as Mike talked and noticed Brian watching her from the other side of the circle, a look of admiration and interest in his eyes. Quickly she averted her eyes.

"Next on the agenda are Sabbath nature scenes," Mike said. "Split up, two by two, and construct any kind of scene you want to with whatever you can find, as long as the scene illustrates a spiritual concept of some kind."

The campers and staff scattered across the area. The twins worked together on the east bank of the spring. Donnie asked Brian to construct a scene with him at the edge of the scrub. Todd and Sandy claimed the area beside the buckboard.

Tory realized as each of the group members paired up that she and Mike were the only ones left without partners. The head wrangler grinned at her, his eyes twinkling. "Come on, let's put them all to shame." He whispered his idea in her ear.

Mike let her pick the spot for their scene. She chose an open sandy area near the corral. A field of wildflowers bobbed in the sunshine nearby. Tory picked a large bouquet of the colorful blooms and placed them on the sand.

Next she gathered twigs, pebbles, and leaves of varying shades of green. Together, they fashioned a picture of an eagle in full flight using the flower petals and leaves. Tory used the twigs to form the words, "Soar with the Spirit" under the eagle.

The last twig in place, Mike stood back and admired their handiwork. "Great job, kid." He smiled proudly at her.

"You, too, boss," she grinned.

The others were finishing up their projects, too. Mike called everyone together again to tour the scenes and allowed each pair to explain the spiritual significance of what they had created.

The twins had built two small altars. One had a bundle of white horsehair resting on top. The other held a small pile of raisins and banana chips. Two stick figures stood in front of the horsehair altar.

Connie explained to the group that the stick figures were Cain and Abel and the altars contained their offerings. "We changed history, though," Carol said. "We had Cain apologize to Abel for being jealous and giving him a hard time."

"Yeah. They're friends again." Connie laughed. "It's much better that way."

Tory slipped an arm around each of the girls and gave them a squeeze. "I love your scene," she said. "Good job, both of you."

Donnie and Brian, in a small clearing by the edge of the woods, had constructed a diorama illustrating the life of Christ. A miniature twig manger held a stick figure baby Jesus, with a flower stalk Joseph and Mary leaning over him. Three crosses stood on a sand hill near the tomb made of mud from the spring bank. A stone fashioned of bark and mud rested to the side of the empty tomb. Tory gasped at the intricacy of their handiwork.

Donnie beamed. "It just seemed like the perfect scene for me to do right now," he told the group shyly. Brian nodded in agreement.

Todd and Sandy stood beside their scene as the group circled around the buckboard. A boat shaped from a palm frond and fastened with twigs rested on the crest of a sandhill. Stick figure animals marched down the side of the hill two-by-two.

"Let me guess," Tory laughed as she linked an arm through Sandy's. "It's obviously Noah's ark after it landed, but what's your spiritual application?"

"The horses made us think of the animals in the ark," Todd explained. "The spring reminded us of the flood. And we divided up two-by-two to do our scenes, just like the animals did." He laughed.

Sandy squatted beside the miniature Mt. Ararat and gazed thoughtfully at her handiwork. "It represents a fresh start, a chance to start over clean and new," she said quietly. "Every day we face a whole new world— new challenges, new learning experiences. God can turn every circumstance into an opportunity for growth, just like this week. We've all grown a lot."

The campers nodded their agreement. Mike moved to the center of the group. "Great job, everyone. Give each other a pat on the back. All of your scenes were thought-provoking and well done. Now, is anybody hungry?"

Brian let out one of his famous war whoops and several of the campers joined him.

Just then a station wagon appeared on the road above the spring. Craning her neck to see who had arrived, Tory heard Sandy squeal as Wally stepped out of the car carrying a huge chocolate cake. Tory's mouth watered just looking at it.

"There's more food in the back," Wally called. He opened a rear door of the car. "Give me a hand with this beanfest everybody."

Tory stared at Mike as Brian and Sandy and several of the campers ran to help unload the food. "You didn't tell us you were bringing Sabbath dinner in. We had planned canned soup for lunch today."

Mike winked at her. "Just a little surprise. I didn't suppose anyone would mind a little alteration in the menu."

Brian walked by carrying a huge bowl of potato salad, a platter of deviled eggs, and a bag of fresh tomatoes. "This is torture," he groaned. "Tory, how about slicing these tomatoes, and lets get this show on the road?"

Sandy lugged a pot of baked beans to the buckboard where she placed it beside Wally's chocolate cake. "Now all we need is lemonade," she teased.

"At your service, my lady," Wally said gallantly and retrieved a large cooler from the car. He pressed the spigot, filled a paper cup with cold lemonade, and handed it to her. "Is there anything else you'd like?"

She shook her head. "No, I think I have everything I need right here."

Mike asked God's blessing on the food, and the

group dug in with enthusiasm.

"You'd have thought we'd been starving them all week," Tory said as she speared a forkful of potato salad. "I guess I will have to admit this is better than our cooking."

Wally laughed. "You should have tasted the food we had on the sailing trip." He grimaced. "Most of us, including Jan, ended up with diarrhea and fever blisters from too much sun. It was a great trip, but I am very glad to be back. And I'm glad they let me deliver the food today." He gave Sandy a sidelong glance. She blushed and turned for a second helping of baked beans.

"I heard something this morning you guys might be interested to know," Wally said, his expression suddenly grave. "Wesley left camp today. He got a phone call from his mom. His dad is dying of cancer, and they think he won't make it through the weekend."

The group fell silent. Tory felt as if someone had punched her in the stomach. So that was it. She'd chalked Wesley's behavior up to a surly personality and bad manners when all this time he'd been attempting to deal with a load of grief.

"Let's pray for him," Brian said quietly. His prayer was simple and sincere, requesting comfort for Wesley and his family and courage for Wesley's father as he faced death.

Tears rolled down Tory's face as Brian prayed. She thought of her own parents and how devastated she would be if anything happened to either one of them. Finally she made up her mind to send Wesley a card as soon as she got back to camp.

CHAPTER
FIFTEEN

Tory wandered among the tents, watching the campers busy at various tasks. She felt a bond to each one, as if they'd formed a family unit during their week together. A lump began to form in her throat. It would be great to sleep in her comfortable bed back at camp and not smell like horse sweat, but she'd miss these kids.

Mike and Brian built a roaring fire and the group gathered around, singing campfire tunes and swapping stories. Tory sat in the circle watching the firelight dance on each familiar face. Just then, she felt someone touch her shoulder.

Todd stood beside her. The haunted expression had returned to his eyes.

"Can I talk to you, Tory?"

"Sure, Todd. Let's take a walk." She was determined not to let the opportunity slip away. They followed the path that wound around the spring.

"What is it, Todd?" She touched his arm. "I can see that something is really bothering you."

Tears welled up in his eyes. Tory could see them shining in the moonlight.

"It's just that I'm afraid," he said miserably.

"Afraid of what?" She didn't want to pressure him, but she could tell that whatever it was that had tortured him for so long was difficult for him to talk about.

The boy walked silently for a while, then sighed. "I'm afraid God can't forgive me. That I won't ever have a relationship with him like Brian and Mike do. Like Donnie has now."

"God doesn't just forgive, Todd, He *is* forgiveness." She prayed silently for wisdom as she spoke.

Todd shook his head. "But you don't know what I've done." He sat down on a log near the spring and buried his face in his hands. "I know God can't forgive me."

"There isn't anything God can't forgive if you accept His forgiveness, Todd," she urged.

"It happened last year at camp. I slept with this girl. I didn't mean to let it happen—it just did." He sighed. "I know I hurt her a lot. I ignored her the rest of the week and haven't seen her since. What if I have AIDS or some kind of venereal disease?"

He stood and began to pace back and forth in front of the log.

"You know, I really wanted to wait. I wanted it to be special with the girl I married. I know this sounds really weird coming from a guy, but it was really important to me to be a virgin when I got married."

Tory sat silent for a moment, searching for the right words.

"Todd," she said finally, "I'm sorry you've had to go through all this pain. It must have been terrible for you." She paused while he sat back down beside her.

123

"You must believe that God forgives you, that He's holding His hands out to you with His gift of forgiveness and restoration. All you have to do is take it and be healed. Can you do that?"

Todd shivered as a cool breeze blew over the spring. "But how can I undo the damage I've done?"

"You can't," Tory said gently. "But you can make careful choices with your body from now on. You can start over right now to protect that special bonding mechanism until you're married. Remember your ark scene today? There was a message in that for *you*."

Todd sighed. "I would love to start over. Worrying about this has been horrible."

"I can see that on your face." She shook her head. "Doesn't look like fun to me. Would you like to pray about it?"

He nodded silently.

"Father," she prayed, "I ask you to wrap Todd up in your forgiveness so tight that he just rests in your love and lets go of the pain he's been carrying around for a year. I ask for healing for this girl, too. Thank you for your promise that you specialize in new starts. I ask for one for Todd right now. In Jesus' name, Amen."

Todd's voice trembled as he joined in. "I accept your healing and forgiveness, God. Help me from now on. And please help me not to get sick. Amen." Tory put an arm around his shoulder and gave him a hug.

"I have the name of a doctor you can see, Todd. I'll give it to you when we get back to camp. Go in for a checkup. Tell him your concerns. You can trust him to keep it confidential. You need to set your mind at ease so you can go on with your life."

Obvious relief on his face, the boy nodded.

Together they walked back down the path toward camp.

"Why don't you join the others, Todd? It's the last night of the trailride."

He flashed her a grateful smile and reached over to kiss her lightly on the cheek. "Thanks, Tory. You saved me."

"Nope. Not me." She laughed softly. "But you do look like you feel better. Let me know if you ever need to talk again. I'll be rooting for you!"

Tory meandered around the outside of the circle of singing campers until she found a spot to sit slightly apart from the others. She wanted to think over what had just happened but still be close to the group.

The campfire popped and crackled, its flames casting dancing shadows on the tents. The moon hung over the spring like a giant night-light, shining on the horses' backs as they milled in the corral. Tory could see Mayonnaise's silver mane glistening.

Mayonnaise.

She tried to imagine going back to laundry tubs and wringer washers. To dirty socks and hot dryers. The workouts on Mayonnaise had been in preparation for the pack trip. Would she even be welcome at the barn now that she was no longer needed?

Just then she sensed someone's presence beside her and looked up to see Brian standing in the firelight.

"May I sit down?" he asked.

Tory scooted over to make room. "Sure. What's up?"

Brian sat down close beside her. She could smell his aftershave and tried to identify it. Old Spice, maybe? The warmth of his arm next to hers distracted her. Her thoughts tumbled over one another in confusion. Although she tried to think of a witty comment to make, her mind was blank, so she just sat in silence until he spoke.

"I wanted to tell you how good I think you are with the kids. Mike and I have been talking about you. You're great with the horses, too." He shook his head and laughed. "You broke that paint gelding in record time. I'm impressed."

"Thanks. That's a nice compliment. It was fun. The whole pack trip's been fun."

"Sure has been." He rubbed his chin thoughtfully. "We'd like you to come back next year, Tory. Mike asked me to mention it to you."

"On the pack trip? Great!"

"No. Not just the pack trip. For the whole summer as a regular staff member. A wrangler. To train the young horses, take trail rides out, help with the rodeos. It's hard work, but Mike seems to think you'd be up to it, and I'd have to say from what I've seen, I agree with him."

Tory felt as if her heart had stopped. She wiped her clammy palms on her jeans and took a deep breath. A wrangler. In the stables. For the whole summer. It seemed too good to be true.

She felt his work-roughened hand slip over hers. The world became a blur of voices, sounds, and smells. She tried to pull herself back to reality but all she could focus on was the warmth of his hand on hers and the sparkle of his eyes in the moonlight.

"What do you say, Tory?" he asked. "Mike would like you to keep working Mayonnaise the rest of this summer, too, if you want to."

"Yes," Tory blurted, trying to keep her voice from shaking. "Yes, I really would like to do that!"

He breathed a sigh of relief and squeezed her hand. "Great. It'll be a good summer. I can feel it in my bones."

She could feel his eyes on her face, studying her.

"You know, Tory," he said softly, "you're really pretty. You're different from a lot of other beautiful girls I know. Yours seems to come from somewhere deep inside. Do you know what I mean?"

Tory thought of her talk with Connie and nodded. "Yes, I think I do." Embarrassed, she grinned. "Thanks."

Brian laughed. "Thank *you*. I'm the one who gets to look at you."

Tory thought of Jan and smiled to herself. She knew her days of envying her were part of the past. It felt great to be able to think of her without feeling jealous. Brian glanced at her quizzically.

"What are you smiling about?"

"Oh nothing. Just enjoying being me." She squeezed his hand. "And enjoying being with you."

She closed her eyes. This pack trip had been the best week of her life. The idea of working full time in the barn almost overwhelmed her. Of working with Mike. And with Brian. Instead of one week's adventure, it would be a whole summer. A real *wrangler* summer.

Tory felt something pressed into her hand. When she opened her eyes, she saw Todd standing over her. He had given her a bouquet of wildflowers.

Grinning mischievously, he said, "For the prettiest horsewoman I know. You look like these match your mood tonight."

Tory laughed. "Yes they do, as a matter of fact. They do indeed."

She smiled at Brian as she slipped a daisy in her hair.